Andrew,
Happy Birthday
Goose!!
Love Sophie.
(Momma Goose).

*For as long as there have been humans.*

*There has been fear.*

*As long as there has been fear.*

*There have been Legends.*

*And with each Legend.*

*There have been monsters...*

*Age of*
# VAMPIRES

SOPHIE PETFORD

*In loving memory of my father – Neil Petford.*
*A man who will 'remain in all our hearts,*
*Forever and Always.'*

# AUTHOR'S NOTE

*Music has always been a powerful, motivational, inspirational force that has pushed me through my life, ranging from 'Bon Jovi' through to 'Black Veil Brides'. No matter what the genre, the music I have listened to has always been that light in the darkness, that supportive voice when everyone else said I would fail at something. This novel is physical proof of the effect that music has had on me. This book was not made to make me rich nor was it to get me a lot of attention: It was to help others. Some of Lucy's experiences within this novel are almost identical to ones that I have experienced personally, so as you read this book, know that you are reading a piece of my soul. To anyone who is reading this and can relate to any events or have experienced similar battles to those within this book, know this: You are never alone and life always gets better. Keep fighting.*

Sophie Petford

'When people hurt you over and over, think of them like sandpaper. They may scratch and hurt you a bit, but in the end you end up polished and they end up useless.'

Andy Biersack

'Good judgement comes from experience. Experience comes from bad judgement.'

Jim Horning

# PROLOGUE

At first glance Lucy Brown would appear to be a normal girl, a little on the gothic side; sporting long, dark hair, heavy eyeliner and a leather jacket, but apart from that, no-one would look at her twice while walking down a crowded street.

Except she was *not* normal: Quite the contrary – She was a broken individual, with a past full of darkness, loneliness, death, and disappointment.

This is her story of how one secret led to another, how her dreams came true, how she suffered even more despair and heartbreak, and ultimately, how she died.

# CHAPTER ONE

I t was that day again...
    The anniversary of their deaths.

I sighed to myself, silencing my alarm as I laid back on my burgundy sheets, staring at the plain ceiling of my room.

I frowned, closing my eyes "C'mon girl. It's just another day." I muttered to myself "Just another day."

Although a bright ray of sunlight shone through a small space between my curtains, I couldn't feel its warmth as my skin was ice cold, filled with the dread of facing the world that day.

I slowly pushed away my covers and sat upright, turning to hang my legs off the side of the bed as my eyes caught sight of their familiar faces: Both of which were contained within silver plated picture frames. Within those frames they were safe, ageless, and happy. That was the beauty of photographs; they never faded, unlike memories and people; they were constant, immortal objects, holding small moments of different people's lives, bringing a fraction of joy to the bereaved families that they left behind. With one glance at the mixture of colours and shapes that made up my father and twin sister, hundreds of memories flashed through my mind, reminding me of how perfect our lives were before their premature deaths, and how much I had lost.

I placed my head in my hands and was almost immediately startled by a second alarm buzzing from my phone.

"Alright! I'm up!" I yelled at it, standing upright and grabbing the thin piece of metal and glass and throwing it hard at my bed, only to immediately regret it as it bounced off the mattress and onto the carpeted floor.

"Come *on*." I groaned, retrieving it from the ground and unlocking it, selecting the music section.

I absent-mindedly scrolled through the numerous albums but I knew full well what I was going to choose: I was just trying to distract myself and waste time.

After finally scrolling through all twenty four of my albums, I came to rest on 'Hearts of the Broken' by 'Your Last Goodbye'. A small smile slowly formed on my face as I walked over to my desk and placed my phone onto the docking station. The second the device made contact with it, the sound of a loud, screaming guitar and a heavy drum beat could be heard.

"Oh yeah." I nodded, the smile on my lips widening.

After leaning against my desk for a couple of seconds, absorbing the music, I took a deep intake of breath and stood upright. "Okay. Let's do this."

Grabbing my hairbrush, my make-up bag and some clothes from my wardrobe, I walked into my en-suit bathroom.

Throwing my shorts and night top back onto my unmade bed, I walked over to my leather rucksack, grabbing my school equipment from my desk. The desk that still harboured my phone, which continued to blare out a loud, heavy rock song, full to the brim of aggressive guitar solos, complicated, loud drum patterns and a deep, smooth, masculine voice.

"Right, time to go." I muttered to myself, throwing my bag over one shoulder and grabbing my leather jacket. I paused the music on my phone, proceeding to pocket it and the black headphones which were next to the docking station. Finally, before I left I grabbed my car keys from a small, ceramic bowl next to the photos of my sister and father, which were situated on my bedside table.

"Bye mum!" I shouted as I descended the stairs, on my way to the door.

"Hey Lucy! Breakfast!" She demanded from the kitchen.

"Nope, no time – I need to pick Tom up." I replied, lacing my boots up.

She appeared in the doorway of the lounge, her hand on her hip.

"Fine. But take this." She produced a red apple from behind her back and handed it to me.

"Alright thanks mum, love you!" I grabbed the fruit before racing out of the door and onto the drive. I stuck the apple in my mouth to free one of my hands, and I unlocked the car, proceeding to toss my jacket and bag into the back before quickly jumping into the driver seat.

I pulled out my phone to check the time and it read 8:50am.

"Crap." I muttered to myself after taking a bite out of the apple and storing the piece, like a hamster, in the side of my mouth as I slammed the car door.

I raced down the surprisingly quiet roads and I arrived at Tom's house to see him waiting for me at the end of the road.

I wound down my window, smiling at him.

"C'mon, get in. Sorry I'm late!"

He shot me back a weak smile and I could tell *immediately* that something was wrong as he walked across the front of the vehicle and opened the door, taking a seat beside me.

Although I knew we were in a rush, I didn't start the ignition and I turned to look at him, one eyebrow raised.

"Spit it out." I demanded, noting his tired, uncomfortable expression.

"Lucy..."

"Go on Tom. I am having a bad enough day as it is, I do not need you, *my boyfriend,* who is meant to be supportive and helpful, being extremely mopey and wasting both of our time. C'mon. Out with it."

He took a deep breath and said quickly "I think we should break up."

My eyes widened. "Excuse me?!"

"I think we should break up, Lucy..."

*Ouch.*

"Where did this come from?!" I demanded, a hurt anger edging into my voice.

He shook his head. "I don't know... I mean... Alice-"

I cut him off. "Alice... Alice Collins, my *best friend* Alice? Are you serious?!"

He nodded, bowing his head in shame.

"Wow... Just wow." I stared him down. "Oh and by the way Tom? Today is the anniversary of my dad and Helena's death, alright? So thanks for making a crappier day even worse. Get the hell out of my car."

He opened his mouth to say something, but I interrupted him, yelling "OUT!", pointing the way he had come.

He nodded, grabbing the handle and closing the door gently behind him, beginning to walk down the path, his broad, athletic frame becoming smaller by the minute.

"Oh God." I muttered to myself. "Nice going genius." I shook my head and grabbed my phone angrily, choosing a loud, aggressive song with loud vocals and intricate guitar solos.

I started the ignition in time with the music and I stalled the car.

"Come ON!" I yelled at it, slamming my hand on the side of the steering wheel. "I do *not* need this!"

I once again turned the key, but to no avail.

"You've got to be kidding me..." I tossed the keys on to the passenger seat in anger and picked up my phone, calling the breakdown services.

*Ring ring. Ring ring. Ring ri–*

"Hello, this is Suzanne at –"

"Yeah, I know where I'm calling to." I snapped "My car just broke down on Briorcreek Avenue, Westwood, I am late for school and I am having a *really* bad day, can you get someone down here?"

There was a brief pause on the other end of the phone before the woman replied with "Yes, we will get someone to your location as soon as possible."

"Cheers." I said shortly, before hanging up and banging the back of my head against the headrest, letting out a deep breath.

My music returned as few seconds later and I let it flood my mind, blanking everything else out.


You know when breakdown companies say 'As soon as possible'? Yeah. They don't mean *as soon as possible.*


I sat waiting in my car for a good *hour* before the useless people arrived and even then all they did was jump start my vehicle and tell me to be on my way.

I put my key in the ignition and sure enough, it started.

I sped off, only slowing down after looking at my speedometer, realising that I was almost speeding with some important people following me.

I looked down at the time on my phone and groaned, *knowing* that I would be extremely late: 10:05am.

"Lovely."

I attempted to keep my cool as I was stuck behind an extremely slow driver, doubling the duration of the journey to school.

The second I pulled into the car park I tugged at my keys, shoving them in my back pocket. I paused my music and then turned around in my seat to grab my bag and jacket before leaving the car.

I slammed the door behind me, locking it immediately and I quickly ran to the front entrance, tugging my jacket on, only to be met by the broad, tall, balding head–master who constantly appeared to be in a bad mood.

"Miss Brown!" He growled at me, in a low, cold, voice. "Why are you late?"

I sighed. "Sir, I–"

"*Why* are you late?" He repeated, cutting me off.

"I was trying to tell you..."

"Don't answer me back." He replied sharply, narrowing his eyes at me. "Unless you *want* to end up in detention?"

I took a deep breath in an attempt to hold my tongue "No sir."

"Will you tell me why you are late?"

"Yes sir."

He waited impatiently, crossing his arms.

"My car broke down and the services took over an hour to get there."

He smirked at me "What, did you stall it with your awful woman driving?"

His response was no surprise to me as it was common knowledge that this man was a chauvinistic pig.

"No sir." I replied, clenching my jaw.

"Well get yourself off to class and don't do it again." He warned, obviously already bored with lecturing me.

"Thank you sir." I replied sarcastically and before he could say anything else I had set off down the corridor.

"Asshole." I muttered to myself, while walking towards my next lesson of English and just being my luck, it was situated at the opposite end of the school.

I rounded the corner and saw Harry Anderson leaning against the wall with two of his other 'henchmen'.

"You've *got* to be kidding me." I sighed.

"Oh look it's Vampire girl!" He exclaimed, noticing me.

"Lay off, Harry." I Replied, clenching my jaw.

Ignoring me, he continued with his taunting. "Oh, you look *angry* Lucy? I heard you and your boyfriend broke up this morning: I bet you're really sad." He continued with mock sympathy and I stopped in front of him, raising an eyebrow.

"Are you done?"

His eyes lit with an unnerving fire and he grinned maliciously. I ignored it and began walking away.

"Also isn't today the day that your sister died? Three years ago?"

I froze mid-step and took a sharp intake of breath, as if being struck by a hard blow in the stomach.

He latched onto the break in my defence and continued "Yeah, you went crazy! Didn't she boys!" He looked between the two sneering, muscular boys at his side.

"Stop." I demanded, my voice cracking slightly and I didn't turn round, fearful of showing the pain on my face.

"Oh and it's dear old *daddy's* death day too!"

This forced me into a fit of rage and I tossed my bag down on the floor and launched myself at him, punching him squarely in the face.

"I said. STOP!" I shouted, seething.

He recoiled at my attack and it took him a few moments to regain his composure. The two students who stood beside him backed away, eyeing me with caution.

When Harry realised what had happened, he grabbed me by the front of my jacket.

"Did you really just do that?"

I looked him right in the eyes and said "Yes." through gritted teeth. Harry posed no threat to me and I did not fear him, although I had been on the receiving end of his brutality on more than one occasion.

"Well" He began, tightening his grip on my jacket "that was your *big* mistake."

"Oh really?" I met his angered, threatening gaze with a slow smile as I brought my right knee up and struck him straight between the legs.

He released me immediately and doubled over in pain, letting out a tortured groan.

"I said stop." I repeated, shrugging my shoulders and backing away, retrieving my bag and once again walking down the corridor.


"Do you not know when to stop?" Came an unknown, masculine voice from behind me.

I frowned and turned, confused at the new voice that had entered that seemingly dead conversation.

I then realised that Harry was stood only mere metres away from me and he had now turned to face the newcomer who had just addressed him.

"Who the hell are you?" Harry asked gruffly.

"That wasn't what I asked." The voice once again sounded, its body still concealed by Harry's large figure.

I edged around him and my eyes fell upon an extremely attractive, brunet boy around 5ft 8 with a perfectly chiselled jaw bone.

"Lucy got in the way." Harry responded, obviously annoyed at his interruption.

"Lucy?" He tilted his head around Harry to look at me.

"Hey Lucy, I'm Lucien."

A mocking smile formed on Harry's lips "Oh look Lucy! A Vampire name! You two should get on really well."

Lucien raised an eyebrow at his petty attempt at an insult.

"Wow." He replied, looking at him as if he was an uneducated child. "I'm gonna go now. Lucy, do mind if I join you? I'm probably going to die from the lack of intelligent conversation with this guy."

I nodded, immediately warming to the mysterious newcomer. "Sure."

"Great." He flashed me a perfect smile as he walked past Harry, who was still trying to think of something relevant to respond with.

Lucien and I continued to walk down the corridor, not looking back to see if Harry was pursuing us or if he had returned to the two other boys.

"So you're new?" I asked him, tilting my head. "I haven't seen you before."

He nodded "Yeah I'm new, I recently moved here from Transylvania." He replied, nonchalantly.

I frowned. "What?"

He broke out into a grin "Sorry, I heard him say something about Vampires." He followed it up with a chuckle.

"Oh right I get it, tease the 'Vampire girl'." I replied, rolling my eyes and shaking my head.

"Why do they call you that?"

Obviously I couldn't tell him the *truth* so I merely regurgitated the cover story which I had told to everyone who asked, shrugging.

"I find them fascinating. I just quite like the idea of a 'higher being' that can blend in with people, hidden in plain sight."

"I thought they were obvious to see? With the capes and stuff?"

I laughed "Nah, that's Bram Stoker thinking. I'm on about the newer stuff." I quickly added "But anyway, they're just myths. It's impossible for them to be real."

9

He responded with a nervous laugh "Yeah, I guess so."

I frowned at him and bell to mark the end of the first lesson resounded around the hallway.

Before I could even attempt to continue our conversation, I heard the rapid *click click click* of high heels.

I turned around to meet a bouncy, excited, curly haired blonde. "Hey Alice."

"Lucy!" She pulled me into a one armed hug, bending at the waist rather than coming closer to me. "I found out what happened! Ohmygod! Are you okay?"

I nodded, remembering Tom's break-up speech from this morning. "I'm coping."

Although I wasn't. Not because I was entirely heartbroken, but because I felt as though I had lost yet *another* person, so it was painful for me especially on this day. Tom and I had been good friends before we entered a relationship with each other, but as far as I was concerned both my friendship and my relationship with him had now been ruined. That literally left Alice as my only friend.

It was kind of depressing but I had learnt the hard way that the more people you have around you, the more people that can hurt you. I was aware that this way of thinking had pushed many people away and had obliterated some chances at happiness with potential friends, but I wasn't going to dwell on the past as I had always enjoyed my own company: I was able to have complete control over the situation – No nasty surprises. Alice was more than enough for me anyway because she represented at least ten different people as she was extremely emotional and *always* had a bit of gossip to tell me. It was also obvious that we were opposites in every way, but I think that was what made our friendship more interesting.

"Are you really though?" She squinted her eyes at me, searching for any sign of weakness so that she could latch onto it and 'fix me'.

I gave her a smile "No Alice, I'm alright." I told her, reassuringly, nodding my head.

"Good. It was obvious it was never going to last anyway; He's super popular and really hot."

"What's that meant to mean?!" I replied, offended.

She batted a hand at me "I meant he was a good catch, that's all. Anyway who's the new piece of fresh, hunky meat?" She pointed over my shoulder to Lucien and I rolled my eyes. "That's Lucien, he's new."

She looked him up and down "Mmm, I can see that."

I raised one eyebrow at her "Really?"

"What!"

"*Every* male that walks through that door? Seriously?"

She shrugged "You have to admit, he is hot."

"I suppose."

"Ohmygod! You LIKE him! I am so getting you together! You'd be the cutest couple ever! Yay!" She screamed excitedly, clapping her hands.

"Can you not?" I asked, beginning to walk away.

She trailed me, poking me. "C'mon Lucy! Don't deny that you want a piece of that meat."

"Seriously Alice, you scare me sometimes." I frowned at her as we walked down the corridor.

Classes went smoothly that day, albeit boring, with only a few dirty looks from Harry when he passed me in the hallway. I also hadn't seen Lucien that day either, until the end of school when I was walking towards the exit, ready to get home and just lay down, listen to some music and sleep: Anything to escape the emotions and memories that always accompanied that day.

But alas, I wasn't even allowed that peace as he walked up to me.

"Hey Lucy." He shot me another smile, but this time it held a slight sense of discomfort.

I was about to ask him what was wrong, but I decided against it as I was mentally exhausted and extremely looking forward to going home.

"I have something to tell you…"

I sighed, closing my eyes. "Can it please wait until tomorrow Lucien? I really can't, not today."

"But-"

"Please. Just give me today. It was nice meeting you and thank you for helping me with Harry, but I need some time to myself."

He nodded understandingly.

"Alright. I'll see you tomorrow. I hope you're alright." He shot me a sympathetic smile.

I was sure that one of the other students had told him what today meant to me, or perhaps he had overheard Harry's taunts from the morning, either way I didn't care. Not today.


I slowly made my way over to my car and when I arrived I looked at it, raising an eyebrow.

"Wow... That is pretty impressive." I said sarcastically to myself as I noted how haphazardly I had parked the vehicle.

"Ah well." I muttered to myself, unlocking the door and opening it.

As I bent to get in the car, a nagging pain shot up my spine and I winced and frowned.

"Ow." I muttered to myself. Where the hell had *that* come from?

Shaking my head dismissively, I tossed my bag and jacket onto the passenger seat and lowered myself into my own seat.


Throughout the car journey home my back kept twitching with pain, but it had felt more like an ache rather than anything serious, so I simply ignored it.

As I was indicating to turn left at the junction to my road, my eyes were drawn to the right - The direction of the graveyard.

I sat there for a few moments, my eyes still focussed on the church spire that I could faintly see in the distance, and I changed my indicator to suggest that I was turning right.

I had decided to visit my father and sister. Although they were gone, they were *certainly* not forgotten. I had mourned them for years, crying at the loss of their lives from this world, yet I could still smile at the memories their names brought to mind. They caused my heart to bleed with a tortured pain, yet they were the ones who could also fix it – Seeing their faces in photographs, the images not having been distorted by the feelings of despair that plagued my mind like a disease.

The photographs were unmoving, unchanging, solid pieces of information that no matter how much time passed, never faded, never lied, and never let me down. Seeing their faces every day when I woke up, smiling at me from my bedside table, made it slightly easier to deal with my life without them.

Yet as I stared at their names, engraved into the mercilessly unyielding, cold, white marble that marked their passing, I couldn't help but feel the dread once again descend upon my soul. The distant memories of those tortured, lonely nights, filled with horrifying nightmares of them being killed in different ways, or even witnessing the *true* way they had died and being helpless to stop it – Merely watching on in distraught despair at the car crash that ended my father's life; Watching it in what seemed like slow-motion; seeing his face as he saw the intoxicated driver speeding down the road in the wrong direction; watching the horror enter his eyes as he knew that it was the end, his end... and then waking up screaming, crying, begging for his return. But those pleas were simply met by the mocking, deafening sound of silence, reminding me that I am truly, indefinitely, alone.

Then there was Helena: My twin sister and best friend.

The only thing that accompanied her name in my mind's inspiration for nightmares was a big, bold, barbed question mark.

Her death was from unknown causes.

Her body's whereabouts were unknown.

So instead of giving me a single moment of rest, my mind decided that my fate was to imagine every single possible outcome of how she could have died, such as:

A brutal murder after which someone stole her body and discarded it into a river in which her once pale, flawless skin now supported jagged, rough blade marks that ruined any features that once defined her. Her soft, clean complexion now plagued by rotting flesh, half eaten by the living organisms that haunted her final resting place. Her amber flecked, hazel eyes that we had both been born with, nothing more than empty, glazed over, dead orbs – The light that once resided in them, the *spark* that made her who she was, gone.

My sister was dead. Those four words constantly reverberated around my soul, coated in a sharp, barbed shell, destroying me from the inside out. Everywhere I looked all I could see was her absence:

My room – We used to spend hours sprawled over every surface, varying styles of music blasting around the four walls, accompanied with our voices and laughter. Those walls that once reflected light, happiness and good memories, now only held the reflection of loneliness, and the cold abyss that resides in my heart where Helena used to be. She wasn't just my sister: She was the one person who never abandoned me, always supported me and was the one who promised that she would be there forever.

But just like everyone else, she had broken her promise.

Just like everyone else, she abandoned me.

Just like every single other person who I had EVER let in to my life, she left me with tears in my eyes and a hole in my heart.

A searing anger coursed through my blood as I stared at their names, my eyes clouding with burning tears that proceeded to cascade down my face as I fell to my knees in front of them.

"YOU'RE JUST LIKE EVERYONE ELSE!" I yelled, my heart broken anew.

"YOU ABANDONED ME!"

I felt the agony of my heart being once again crushed as I fell to the ground onto my side and sobbed hard into the dry grass.

"You left me." I whimpered, curling tightly into myself, shutting out the rest of the world. I surrendered to the despair that had once again attached itself to their names and forced its way like a cold snake through my mind, seizing each and every positive thought and squeezing the life from it, crushing it and turning it to dust, pushing me further and further into the darkness that was my unconscious mind: A place that held only horror, misery, and loneliness.

This was why I never became attached to anyone. *This* was why I never cared: Because when I cared I could be hurt. I was tired of letting people in and them inadvertently or maliciously, destroying me from the inside out, abandoning me, using me, betraying me and breaking my soul further, adding another crack to the almost shattered figure that was my mind.

So now I was cold.

Now I was withdrawn from the world.

I had only my mother, Alice, and myself to keep me company.

Of those three people, the only person that I could ever rely on, the only person I could ever truly trust was myself.

I was my lifelong companion. I was the only one who would never abandon me. Although on many occasions, I wished that I could. I wished that I could just lose my fractured, broken mind and become an empty, cold shell, sat alone in a darkened room.

I wished that I no longer had to feel the pain.

The pain of life.

But I did.

I slowly raised myself from the ground, tears staining my cheeks and an emotionless, dead expression resting on my face as I once again looked to their names.

'Richard Steven Brown.'

'Helena Rose Brown'

My distant eyes moved further down the gold letters.

'Tragically killed.'

'Tragically lost.'

Drifting past their ages, my eyes fell upon the short message that resided at the bottom of both headstones.

'In our hearts,

Forever and Always.'

'Forever'... 'and'... '*Always.*'

My thoughts fell to those permanent words that had been tattooed onto the flesh on the back of my right shoulder, constantly reminding me of those I had lost, keeping them with me forever.

My eyes once again flashed between their names and the last line that marked their existence on this earth.

I repeated this action until I felt myself coming back from the edge.

I felt as though a thick, invisible, suffocating blanket had been removed from my mind – The world once again regained colour, the sound of birdsong returned to my ears, and I could breathe without each inhalation being ragged and sore, brushing up my dry, coarse throat like sandpaper on an open wound.

I could look away from their gravestones without it feeling like a dagger being slowly dragged across my eyes, and I could think rationally once again.

Letting out a deep, freeing breath, I knelt down in front of the pale marble and forced a small, pained smile to cross my face.

I reached to my father's name and traced my fingers around the letters, letting out a deep sigh, bowing my head and closing my eyes.

Slowly opening them again, I lowered my hand and turned my head to my sister's gravestone: The one that had no body to represent. I stared at it for a few moments before standing once again and backing away a couple of steps.

"I love you." I said quietly, looking slowly between their names before turning, my head bowed, as I walked back to my car that would transport me home.

# CHAPTER TWO

T he following morning I awoke with a sharp burning pain that stretched from a point between my shoulders, down to the middle of my back.

Wincing, I slowly sat up, reaching behind me and rubbing the source of the discomfort, attempting to massage the pain away. Without much success I rose from my bed and walked towards my full body mirror. As I neared the reflective surface, I noticed a change in my appearance: I saw that my eyes appeared more sunken, the dark circles seeming to be more prominent, framing my eyes with a look of exhaustion. While gazing upon my tired reflection, I recalled that the small journey from my bed to the mirror had caused me pain - my joints had felt extremely sore and weak. Testing this theory, I shrugged lightly and a small aching pain flashed across my shoulders causing me to wince.

I dismissed this pain as the aftermath of my breakdown within the graveyard the previous day, and I continued with my morning routine. After locating a pair of black fitted jeans, my band shirt for 'Your Last Goodbye', my make-up bag, and my phone, I resumed the song that I had been listening to the day before as I entered my en-suit to get ready for school.

Once I was dressed, I re-entered my room, closing the bathroom door behind me. I removed my phone from my front pocket and saw that the time was only 8:15am. Realising that I was actually early for once, I made my way over to my bed and withdrew a thick book from a drawer in my bedside table.

'A History of Vampires – The Chronicles of the Undead'

I sat cross-legged on my bed and lost myself for an unknown amount of time within the words that my brain hungrily absorbed, searching for an answer to the question that had been plaguing my mind for the past three years:

'Was it possible?'

I jumped at the sound of my mother entering my room and calling my name.

I looked up quickly and she smiled, another red apple in her hand.

"I'm guessing you're going to need this: It's quarter to. Get going Lucy."

I looked down at my phone and saw that she was correct: If I didn't leave now, I would be late. Again.

I replaced my black, tasselled bookmark between two crisp pages and left the book on top of my burgundy bed sheets, grabbing my school bag, headphones and keys as I started towards the door.

My mother held out the apple in her pale, manicured hand. Taking it from her, I noted that over the past year she had acquired quite a likening to the colour red: Both her nails and lips were painted crimson and she constantly wore a small ruby necklace. I never knew what had caused the sudden change in interest, but I had just ignored it – I liked black clothes and she liked red: It was all just preference.

Or so I thought.


"Today is going to be better." I muttered to myself as I lowered my body gingerly into my seat, my back having become a little more painful, the

20

ache having turned from a slight annoyance to a presence that was certainly prominent in the forefront of my mind.

"Yesterday is over... I'm safe for another twelve months." I reassured myself, forcing a small smile to my lips.

I placed my keys into the ignition and set off to school, attempting to prepare myself for yet another day of boring classes that were *so* important to my future.

Except I had no idea what my future held for me.

As far as I was aware I could die tonight, not having used a single piece of information that I had gleaned from the institutionalised building that was my school.

As far as I was concerned the future was a liquid, nothing was concrete and nothing was certain. You could never plan ahead and you could never rely on something happening because the world will always inadvertently work against your happiness.

Happiness is a desire that people strive to have but never end up achieving, having lived their life wanting more but never getting it, never cherishing what they have. That was the flaw in humanity: Greed. – Never being satisfied with what they have, needing more. Be it money, possessions, or attention. No single person would ever be happy because happiness doesn't truly exist.

A person may delude themselves to think that in their current state of mind they are 'happy', be it a promotion within their job, the birth of their child or winning the lottery, but then look back a day later. They will undoubtedly be wanting something else, desiring something they do not have. So their version of happiness is simply a small moment of satisfaction from one of their infinite number of desires coming true.

Happiness is not a constant emotion and it never will be, not in the eyes of a human – the species that is at the top of the food chain, has control over this world yet continues to destroy everything around them, simply to gratify their own simple desires.

That was why I didn't plan ahead. That was why I had no idea of my future.

I would take things as and when they came because if there was anything I head learnt from the passing of two of my closest family members, it was that anything can happen; your life can be changed in the blink of an eye; your body could fail at any moment, it could generate a single cancerous cell and that would be the beginning of the end for you. The future is uncertain and there's no way to ever make your survival definite. Everyone dies at some point, be it at an hour old, or one hundred years later.

Everyone dies.

This principle has been present since the dawn of time yet the passing of someone still leaves an unholy amount of pain residing with the loved ones left behind. You'd think the human race would be used to death by now, you'd think we would have grown accustomed to it. But that is not the case: We are weak creatures who claim to be the superior species yet one harsh word can evoke such rage within people and one mistake can destroy hundreds of lives. So we are not the alphas of this world.

Which means something else is; something which is strong, powerful, and can overcome anything; something to which time means nothing, 'aging' being merely a word; a superior species that will change the world for the better, not poison it with selfishness and greed.

The age of man is coming to an end, and something is about to take its place.

I had had thoughts like this many times over the past three years: Always feeling that something was wrong, never fitting in and never feeling that I never truly belonged. I began questioning everything I came across and I lost my faith in people and objects as time progressed.

Everything seemed to change and nothing was constant. The only people that I had ever let into my life had either died or used me, always having an ulterior motive: My friendship and company never being enough.

I was lost in my thoughts as I turned the corner and almost missed the brunet, tall, muscular boy walking in the opposite direction along the path.

I slowly pulled up next to him and he turned his head, satisfying my suspicion that it was in fact Lucien. I waved my hand, indicating for him to enter the vehicle.

He lowered himself into the seat and looked at me.

"Thanks for the lift."

"No worries." I responded quietly, returning my gaze back to the road and accelerating.

I knew it was coming.

When someone says 'I need to tell you something' it is *never* good, and I didn't need bad pieces of information in my life at the moment. I didn't need any more people delivering difficult news... today was for me to heal, kind of like the day *after* a funeral when everyone leaves you alone, no-one attempts to comfort you, and you are left by yourself to cope with the pain that flooded your system the day before. So today I just wanted to have one day without something bad happening, but unfortunately it seemed as though I could not have that one simple wish as Lucien started with "Like I said yesterday, I need to talk to you."

I closed my eyes briefly and sighed.

"What about? When someone says that, I never want to know the topic."

He was quiet for a moment and I could see out of the corner of my eye that he was frowning, not looking at anything in particular, appearing to be torn about something.

He shook his head and responded with "Actually, I'm not sure. What I am about to tell you is, yes, a delicate subject–"

I quickly shot him a warning look, before returning my gaze back to the road.

"–But it may also be the best thing you have heard in a long time."

I turned my head and frowned at him.

"What?"

"I suggest you pull over, Lucy." He pointed to a space that was a short distance up the road.

"We need to get to school–"

"Trust me. Do it." He interrupted sharply.

Detecting a sense of urgency in his voice, I did as he suggested and brought the car to a stop.


Once I had turned off the engine, I looked at him expectantly.

He held my gaze momentarily before tearing his eyes away and leaning back in his seat, looking out of the window.

As I was about to push him for information, he let out a deep breath and said "Tell me about the Vampires."

"Excuse me?"

Now he turned his gaze to me and it was a hard, serious one.

"Tell me about the Vampires." He repeated, his pale blue eyes staring into my hazel ones.

I looked away and decided to play whatever game he was conducting.

"They interest me." I said, shrugging.

"No." He responded shortly, once again locking his eyes onto mine.

"No?"

"No, that is not the reason you have researched them for the past three years."

I dismissed any thoughts that suggested he knew my secret and I stuck to my story.

"Yes, it is." I replied through gritted teeth, defending my corner, slightly angered at his confrontation.

"I'm not fighting you Lucy. I know, and you know I do."

I wasn't going to let him get under my skin, so I simply turned in my seat and leaned against my door, facing him.

"Oh really? What makes you think you know so much about me? I met you only yesterday. Just because you confronted the guy that was attempting to give me a hard time, does not give you the automatic right to pretend you know me."

"Lucy." He said, impatiently.

"What."

"Do I really need to spell this out?" He asked, exasperatedly.

"Yeah, I think you're going to have to." I replied, coldly.

He sighed and looked outside the car, checking that no-one else was around.

"Fine." He responded, just as coldly. "You want me to explain myself? You want me to prove that I know your secret? I can do that in just *one* action Lucy. *One*." A hint of anger had crept into his voice and although it was slightly discomforting, I was still determined to defend my corner. This secret was worth a lot to me and I wasn't going to give it up that easily.

"Do it." I demanded.

He tore his gaze from mine, turning his head away from me.

Every hair on my body stood on end as I sensed a change in the atmosphere within the car. Something had changed and every part of my system said '*run*'.

Like normal, I ignored my instincts and when Lucien turned around, I threw myself back against my door in shock, retreating away from him.

"No." I breathed, staring at the feline fangs that had emerged from his canines and stretched down to just beneath his bottom lip. I slowly, disbelievingly, moved my gaze up his face and saw that his eyes were no longer a piercing blue colour, nor did they have any white remaining in them: They were deathly black from corner to corner, and as I stared into these black orbs, I saw my own, shocked expression.

'No, this is *not* true!'

I had researched Vampires, *begging* for their existence for the past three years, but I don't think I had ever truly believed that they actually existed.

A brief flash of hope crossed my mind, but I quenched it almost immediately for fear that that hope was not deserving of this situation.

Although the emotion was destroyed just as quickly as it had presented itself, it had still occurred so my mind thought back to that split second of elation and belief.

'Helena...'

'NO' I shouted in my own mind, knowing that the possibility of the connection was extremely small, but if I believed it, even for a moment, I knew it would destroy me.

Lucien remained within his Vampiric form as he watched my like a hawk, scouring my face for signs of emotion.

"So I ask you again–" His voice came out slightly muffled "Tell me about the Vampires."

I continued staring at him in shock and when I did not give a response, he continued talking.

"Is it because of Helena?"

Her name being spoken shook me from my reverie and my eyes took on a fiery yet defensive appearance.

"Why would you say that?" I asked quietly.

"Because I know where she is."

The whole world stopped in that instant as his words slowly sunk into my brain.

'He knows where she is... He knows where Helena is... After all this time...'

I suddenly slapped him across the face.

"HOW DARE YOU?!" I roared at him.

He quickly returned back to his human form, the blackness of his eyes withdrawing back into his pupils and his fangs retreated into his normal canines. He gave me a look of pure confusion.

"My sister died three years ago. She was taken from me. I swear to God if this is a joke, I will bloody kill you. No matter *what* you are, I will tear you apart."

He noted the fire in my eyes and even for a Vampire- something that could break my neck in the blink of an eye, he seemed wary of my anger.

"Yes, she did die." He said quietly.

I readied myself for another attack.

"But she came back as one of us." He added slowly.

I once again froze.

It had now been confirmed: My sister still lived.

"She..." I couldn't form any other words, my throat was blocked with the oncoming tears of both shock and relief.

He nodded again. "Yes. Your sister is a Vampire and I know where she is." Lucien's eyes took on a slight sympathetic look, and he gave me a small smile. "She's safe."

"Helena." I breathed, my eyes now welling with tears.

Just as I said her name, a searing pain shot up my spine and I took a sharp intake of breath.

Lucien frowned in concern, but I simply ignored it – I had more important things to deal with, such as seeing my sister.

"Take me to her." I demanded, my voice uneven with the surge of numerous emotions coursing through my system.

He nodded and pointed through the windscreen.

"We need to go to school first."

I frowned, impatient. "No we don't. We need to see my sister."

His face became grim "No, I have to tell Isaac as he was the one who turned her. But yes, we will see her tonight if you wish."

I scowled "Isaac... My music teacher, Isaac? Mr. Carter?"

He nodded. "Yeah. He was told to come here to keep an eye on you."

"But why?"

"Because Helena is your sister and we always get someone to watch those that were left behind, in case they find any information that they shouldn't."

I nodded, understandingly.

"But why do we have to tell him that I know about Helena?"

"Because he is one of the elders and he also needs to 'suggest' to your mother that coming to London with us is a good idea."

I had completely forgotten about my mother for a moment. "I can't tell her... I can't tell my mum that Helena's alive. She's already grieved her and it would kill her to know she's a Vampire."

"She can't know anyway. The only reason you are aware now is because of your research and how adamant you have been with this. When I transformed in front of you a few minutes ago, it was a test: If you had completely lost your mind, I would have wiped everything from your memory, and you would never have even remembered meeting me. But you didn't. Trust me Lucy there aren't actually that many humans who don't run away screaming when we turn."

"But why? You're better than humans in every way; you're immortal; you have the ability to control other people's minds and you have advanced senses... The only reason I acted as I did was because although I had wanted you to exist for the past few years, I never really believed it... Your transformation gave me hope and I was terrified that it had been misplaced." I looked down at my hands speaking quietly, unable to stop myself from talking. "I wasn't scared of you." I looked back up at Lucien, meeting his gaze. "I think Vampires are wonderful. They are everything right that is wrong with this world."

Lucien didn't reply at first, he simply gazed at me in admiration and wonder. "Do you honestly believe all of that?"

"Of course I do. Death terrifies us humans and appearing weak makes us want to prove that we are not. Both of those traits start wars. Humans are a corrupt species whose only aim, as a group, is to destroy everything around them." I still was unable to cease my long speech.

Perhaps because I had kept these thoughts concealed for such a long time, they all flooded out now that I had the chance to truly be honest with someone.

"We kill humans though. We feed on them." He frowned.

I shrugged. "You're higher up the food chain." I responded quickly, not thinking about my answer and afterwards, I felt slightly taken aback and Lucien let out a small chuckle.

"I suppose you're right. Well, I am feeling a little hungry..." He joked.

"Touch me, I dare you. Remember I know everything about you: All your weaknesses, all your flaws. I know every last one." I responded with a sly smile.

Lucien shook his head, his eyes shining with humour at my response. "You really are unique Lucy."

"That's one word for it." I responded, raising an eyebrow briefly, before turning back to face the road.

"We really should get going now. We're late as it is." I checked my phone and saw that I was correct. I had also received a text from Alice.

'Girl! Where you at?! Have you seen Lucien? OMG you're with him aren't you! I know he lives near you but damn that was quick! I'M PROUD! Get your ass to school woman!'

"You whore." I muttered, chuckling at her obvious obsession with any male with a pulse. I laughed harder at the fact that Lucien probably didn't even have a pulse but Alice wanted him anyway.

"Any reason you're laughing hysterically?" Lucien eyed me with slight confusion.

I waved a hand dismissively "Alice thinks you're hot."

"The blonde one? Ah okay."

"Hey she's my friend. Don't knock it."

He held up his hands, surrendering. "I'm not even going to go there."

"Good. Right, because you've made me late, you are going to have to put up with my badass music."

Before he could say anything, I plugged my phone into the car and was met by the familiar sounds of an upbeat song, containing Josh's brilliant guitar, and James's wonderfully deep voice.

Lucien frowned as he listened to the lyrics, seeming to recognise some.

"You like 'Your Last Goodbye'?" He queried.

Lucien knew about the band – I was gaining more respect for Vampires as the seconds passed.

I nodded "Hell yeah."

"Okay cool." A small, sly smile crossed his face, and he attempted to conceal it by looking out of the window.

I shook my head dismissively and looked back to the road, concentrating on the task at hand:

Getting to school and talking to Mr. Carter.


I smiled at the thought of seeing Helena again, feeling as though a heavy weight had been lifted from my soul. Every nightmare that had ever plagued my thoughts about her fate and every lonely hour fell away like broken shackles, freeing me.

I could at least let myself feel a single moment of happiness, knowing that I could see her again.

I swore that I would never again take her presence for granted. Every second with her would be better than the last, filling my mind and driving out every single day of loneliness that I had previously felt due to her absence.


The second I pulled into the car park, I grabbed my phone and my bag, shooting out of the vehicle.

"C'mon!" I groaned impatiently as Lucien slowly got out of the car.

The second I heard the door close, I locked it and began running towards the main building.

I looked back and saw him walking.

"Come *on* Lucien! This is important!"

"Fine." He said, rolling his eyes, and within a second he was by my side, obviously having used his advanced skills.

"Cheat." I muttered.

He shot me a devious grin before putting his arm around my waist and within the next couple of seconds we were at the front doors to the building.

I laughed and took a deep breath, recovering from the new speed that I had just witnessed.

"That's amazing." I breathed, looking at him.

He shot me a smile and winked before walking through the doors.

"Ah, Lucy." My good mood was immediately quenched.

Mr. Atkins -The headmaster- was stood in the centre of the entrance hall, a smug grin residing on his face.

"I see you're late again? This time with another student... You *are* a bad influence."

"Yes, sir." Saying what I could to get him to leave.

"Less of the attitude."

"Okay, sir."

"This is your second day arriving late so I think that values a detention, don't you?"

"No, sir."

"No?"

"No. I'm going to lesson and then leaving school."

He seemed taken aback at my hard remark.

"Excuse me?"

"I am simply here to talk to Mr. Carter and then I'm going." I gave him a sarcastic smile.

I had wanted to talk to him in this way since day one, and Lucien's presence seemed to give me the burst of strength to do so.

"I don't like your attitude Lucy. My office, now."

He began walking away, expecting me to follow. I turned to Lucien.

"Do you mind?" I asked, indicating to the headmaster. "It'll be quicker."

"Yeah, sure." He replied, understanding what I meant.

He quickly walked across to Mr. Atkins and tapped him on the shoulder.

The second he turned to face Lucien, I felt the hair on the back of my neck stand on end and I saw the two men lock eyes.

Lucien quietly muttered something and the headmaster simply nodded and walked away.

"Done." He stated, turning back round to face me, still in his Vampiric form.

My eyes widened briefly at the sudden change, but he reverted back to his human appearance as he returned to my side.

My pulse quickened as I prepared myself to talk to Isaac... He had turned my sister...

It suddenly dawned on me that I didn't know *why* Helena was chosen, but I dismissed the thought as a question to ask him when I saw him.

Lucien and I stood outside Mr. Carter's classroom, and I looked through the thin window in the door. He didn't *look* like a Vampire, but then again neither did Lucien. I mean they were both attractive, but if I thought that every attractive person I came across was a Vampire, life would become a lot more different.

Without any more hesitation, I knocked on the door and he turned around, beckoning us in.

"Hey sir, sorry I'm late."

"Hi Lucy, no worries, is everything alright?" His gaze fell upon Lucien behind my shoulder and he turned to the class.

"I'll be back in a minute."

He made his way across the room and closed the door softly behind him, facing the two of us.

"How can I help?" He asked, looking between our faces.

"She knows, Isaac."

"I thought as much with you both being here together. So, Lucy. How are you taking it all?"

"You know me, sir. I'm loving it." I smiled and added "It was completely unexpected, but you can understand how happy I am."

He nodded in understanding. "Yeah. It killed me, watching you constantly reading about and researching what we are. After seeing you break down on the anniversary last year, I wanted more than anything to tell you that Helena was okay. I'm so sorry Lucy."

I nodded "Yeah. I get it though – laws and things."

"Yeah, you're a human. We're not. Our paths aren't normally meant to cross unless you are about to be turned."

"Which reminds me." I started "Why did you turn her?"

"Ah, I knew this one was coming."

I waited silently for his explanation.

"She had cancer." He said finally.

I frowned. "What?"

This was news to me.

"She had cancer but I took away your memory of it. I also took your mother's too, because of how much it tortured the two of you. Don't worry, the disease isn't hereditary so you're both clean, but there was just something in Helena's system that supported that particular cancer."

"That still doesn't explain why you turned her."

"Before I was told to work here to watch you, I was a doctor at the hospital she was kept in. One day, the disease had spread to almost every part of her body and she begged me for help." His eyes took on a hurt expression as he relived an uncomfortable moment from his past. "She didn't know what I was but she grabbed my hand, her skin as cold as my

33

own, and I could tell she was dying. She was in agony and she begged me for help. Even after all my years on this Earth, I still have a weakness to those who are suffering in front of me. So I helped her. I gave her my blood to heal her and she seemed to be alright, the pain having stopped."

"She told me a Vampire had visited her. She couldn't remember who, because of the pain, but that's why I began researching them." I explained.

"But I took away those memories." Isaac shot me a confused look.

"Not all of them apparently. Me and my mother both knew she was ill, but we didn't know about the cancer. We just thought she was suffering with a normal virus. I came every day after school. One day, she had told me she was better and that a Vampire had healed her. Of course I didn't believe her, but the following day, when she disappeared, I began digging for information."

Isaac nodded gravely. "I was wrong for doing what I did. We rarely work in hospitals, let alone treat cancer patients. Also, we never have the opportunity to save them because patients normally die when we aren't there. This was the first situation that I had ever found myself in where I could cure a patient, suffering from the disease... Or so I thought. The reason that no-one knew about Vampire blood curing cancer, was because it doesn't. That's why she disappeared Lucy. She died." He shook his head, looking away. "I'm sorry. It was wrong of me to do that. I thought I was taking the pain away. But I'm going to be honest with you – It caused even more agony for her. After you had gone home, she started coughing. At first they were just small coughs, and then they got worse: Blood began coming up with each wretch."

I could feel my stomach clenching as he told me this horror story of how my sister had met her end.

"It just got worse and worse. I took her from the hospital and drove her out to a deserted area. I could do nothing but watch her in pain, and it killed me Lucy. I couldn't help her, so I put her out of her misery."

"How?" I asked shortly, feeling lightheaded from the conversation.

34

"I broke her neck." He responded quickly but quietly. "If I had let her bleed out, she would have become a Vampire anyway. That way it was easier and less painful for her. I turned her from a Dhampir into a full Vampire once I had received her consent, after taking her back to London."

"She wanted to be a Vampire?" I questioned.

"Yes. She thought 'why not'. As a Dhampir you don't get heightened senses and you're only a little more powerful than a human. She wanted the 'full package' if she was to live forever."

A small smile crossed my lips. That sounded like her: She didn't like things only half done.

I hesitated before asking "Does she regret it?" I feared that his answer would be yes, and I was scared that Helena would feel trapped. But to my surprise he shook his head.

"Not at all, she actually loves it. Having an immortal love interest doesn't harm that either." He chuckled before adding "She's happy, Lucy. Although on numerous occasions, I have had to console her because of the pain she feels for having left you."

I looked down at my hands for a moment, before responding with "Trust me, it's mutual. At least she knew where I was..."

I trailed off and there was an uncomfortable silence between us before Lucien broke it by saying "But now that's over, and you two are going to see each other again."

A smile returned to my face and I looked at him.

"Yeah. Thank you for telling me today. When can we go and see her?" I quickly turned to Isaac expectantly.

"We'll all travel to London tonight. I'll go and call your mother now and get her to come into school so I can 'explain' the situation to her."

A thought occurred to me "Although I have read a lot about Vampires, just to make sure, mind control is one hundred percent safe, isn't it?"

He smiled and nodded "Yeah, of course. Honestly, all I do is assure her that it's a good idea - She doesn't walk off in a trance or anything."

"Alright, I just needed to make sure ."

He nodded before quickly opening the door and sticking his head through the gap.

"I'll be back in five minutes. Jake, don't break the amps, and Sarah, if you snap the drum stick again you're in detention for a year."

He turned to us, about to walk down the corridor, before spinning back round again, following up with "Oh, and by the way, keep it down - Crazy Atkins is patrolling."

He grinned at us with a glint in his eye "Fear is the best form of persuasion."

I returned his smile for a moment, before it turned into a grimace - I would have previously laughed at that remark, but now that I knew his true nature, what he had said had many different connotations.

# CHAPTER THREE

That day passed at an unholy pace; each minute seeming like an hour; each hour feeling like a day. My excitement built to excruciating heights through the hours, before I had to quench it for the sake my own sanity.

I had tried all that I could to make time go faster:

Reading – The only books I had ever read were about Vampires, and now I no longer needed them because if I wanted to know anything, I could simply ask Lucien or Isaac.

Watching television – Again, my tastes were normally gothic horror, often falling into the Vampire category. I just laughed in mocking discontent at the film writers' attempts at creating the image of a Vampire. Not one film or television show managed to isolate the piercing, pitch black eyes. Also, real Vampire fangs were about double the length of the fake ones used within filming.

That was the end of my list of ideas to distract myself. My mind was blank, and I had no idea what to do.

As I laid back on my bed, sighing, I looked around the room and my gaze fell upon the large, framed poster of the members of 'Your Last Goodbye'. My eyes were drawn to James's face:

His piercing blue eyes, his jet black hair, his porcelain skin and his perfectly defined, structured face. He honestly looked like something that simply couldn't exist. He seemed like a 'higher being' of sorts and he really took my breath away, as did the other band members - They all shared a similar air of power, strength, and intelligence that seemed almost inhuman.

"Maybe they're Vampires!" I chuckled to myself, drawing my eyes away from the picture. Pulling my phone from my front pocket, I selected a slow, quiet song called 'The Eyes of the Soul'. I proceeded to place the device on my bedside table and I laid back on the purple sheets, staring at the ceiling as a slow piano began playing. My eyes drifted closed as I heard James's slow, soothing voice:

> 'I need to see your face once more,
> feel your soul joining with mine,
> hear your voice, calling my name,
> bringing me back from the edge again...'

I felt every muscle in my body relax as the familiar words flooded my mind with a sense of soothing comfort.

That was what I found beautiful about music; it always stayed the same and it never changed; the words remained constant and the feelings they evoked within me, both the sad ones they repressed and the happy ones they blessed me with, simply made me feel like I was not alone. 'Your Last Goodbye' assured me that they cared. Even though their music was listened to by hundreds of thousands of people, it still seemed personal to me.

I recalled writing all of those thoughts down in a letter once and I remembered that on my eighteenth birthday, my mother took me to one of 'Your Last Goodbye's concerts. After the performance I was somehow blessed with meeting James and upon meeting him, I gave him the letter.

I smiled to myself, remembering the extremely fond evening that had been one of the biggest highlights of my life so far.

Thinking back to the event, I recalled how my mother noticed the front of the band's tour van alongside the venue for the concert, but it was so well concealed that no-one else had seen it. So when the members of 'Your Last Goodbye' exited out of the side door, I was the only one there. As they passed, James took my letter that I held out to him, nodded his thanks, and followed the others onto the bus.

I was almost hyperventilating with the excitement that coursed through my veins after he took the paper from me. But with even more crystal clarity, I remembered the small tap on my right shoulder after I had turned around, ready to leave. I turned back around and came face-to-face with James.

It turned out that he hadn't just taken the letter and left, he had actually told the others to wait so that he could talk to me.

I had honestly never felt so special in my entire life – One of the men that I admired the most in this twisted world, actually took time out of his life for *me*: The girl who was deemed a social reject, someone who wasn't even given the time of day by a single person at school, yet also, amazingly, the girl that a musical *legend* decided to talk to.

To this day, I still did not understand my good fortune of that evening.

He began by thanking me, and the second I heard his voice I almost fainted, feeling my face flushing red. It was all I could do to remain standing. The man that stood before me was a kind of *God* to me, and he had been there through each torturous nightmare. In every moment I had believed that I couldn't go on, his voice and the sounds of the other instruments within the band assured me that I could actually continue living and also endure the pain that haunted me daily.

Then there he stood.

After everything the band had done for me, I suppose I didn't really imagine them to be *real* people. So seeing him there in the flesh shook me to my core and made me feel as though I was having the best dream in existence.

After he noticed that I was in a state of shock, he shot me a smile and quickly opened the letter that I had written to him.

I watched his beautiful eyes skimming over each and every word and a few moments later, he folded the paper up and placed it in his inside pocket.

He then just looked at me, not saying a word.

Smiling, he then reached forward, pulling me into a tight hug.

I felt his long arms wrap around me and I suddenly had the breath taken from my lungs: His reaction had been so completely unexpected and it took me a few moments to return the embrace.

He placed his slim chin onto my shoulder and spoke quietly into my ear, assuring me that they would *always* be there, no matter what, and that I should keep the strength that I had worked so hard for.

*That* was when the tears came, but they were silent ones that filled my eyes, spilling down over my cheeks a few moments later.

He sensed my tears and pulled back, looking at me with a concerned expression.

I gave him a watery smile to assure him that I was alright and then, with a shaky breath, I attempted to explain how much what he had just said meant to me.

His warm smile once again decorated his porcelain features and when his eyes locked with mine, I knew then that I was not alone. Their music had helped me so much over the past three years, but that look was something that would remain with me for the rest of my life. It did more than just 'help'- it filled my soul with a sense of belonging. Even though it was possible that I would never meet James again, I would always have this memory and nothing, and no-one could *ever* take it from me.

A screaming fan broke our eye contact as they more or less threw themselves at him. I noticed that the excited individual wasn't an 'individual' at all: I recalled looking around and seeing a massive swarm of people approaching James, all screaming his name excitedly.

He gave the crowd an awkward smile and they all ended up pushing him back towards the steps of his tour bus. That was when I decided to leave.

I locked eyes with him once more and smiled, hopefully giving him an idea of what those short five minutes had meant to me, before I turned and began walking back to the car park where my mother waited.


By the time I had thought through one of the most amazing memories of my existence, the song had ended, and 'Hell's Angel' had begun playing.

I opened my eyes and sat up as I heard the constant drum beat from Chris, the brilliant guitars being played by Damian and Josh, and a few moments later James's deep, aggressive voice joined them:

> 'The fire and brimstone running through my veins,
> The pitch black smoke clouding your face,
> The scorching flames licking the walls of this cell,
> Welcome, my dear, to Hell.'

On the word 'Hell', a fast guitar solo began, accompanied by the loud, rapid, thudding sound of Chris's bass drum.

The second I turned to get off my bed, I heard the music dim and the familiar sound of a text message came through on my phone:

Lucy! Where are you?!

It was Alice. I rolled my eyes and replied with:

Hey, I'm at home – I left school a little earlier.

I almost immediately received a response:

You're home? Good. Come and let me in – I'm outside.

I walked over to my window and looked out of the glass. Sure enough, I could see Alice's smiling face looking up at me, framed by her big, bouncy, blonde curls.

I shook my head, smiling, and threw my phone back onto my bed, proceeding to descend the staircase to open the front door to greet my friend.

Alice barged her way past me and had already begun talking before she had even stepped one foot over the threshold.

"So Tom's been really mopey recently. Pretty sure that's your fault."

I frowned slightly "Oh I'm sorry, does my failed relationship displease you?"

She rolled her eyes at me as I closed the door and she walked up the stairs.

"No, not like that, but thanks to him sulking, the football team are failing."

"Since when do you care about football?"

"I don't, it's a load of meatheads kicking a piece of leather about, but the football team are hot. I cannot date someone who is failing."

Alice had always been concerned with upholding appearances, and that branched out to everything in her life, excluding me it seemed.

"Anyway, how's Lucien?" Her eyes glittered with curiosity and excitement. - This was new news and 'new news' always thrilled her.

I opened my mouth to respond when she entered my room and gave me a look of distaste.

"You've got this music playing again?"

I felt myself tighten in defence.

"Yes, I do."

"Ugh, turn it off."

"No. You know how much they mean to me, Alice. I'll turn it down, but not off. You should have gathered by now that you can't have me without them."

She once again rolled her eyes. "Fine, whatever! Just because I love you Lucy."

"Love you too, Alice." I responded, a hint of annoyance in my voice.

As she requested, I begrudgingly lowered the volume of the music. Even then it seemed like it still wasn't enough judging by the look of disgust on Alice's face, but I just ignored her and sat cross-legged on my bed.

Throwing her bag on the floor, she jumped excitedly next to me and began ribbing me for information.

"So. Lucien!"

"What about him?"

"Is he good in bed?"

"Excuse me?!" I responded, wide eyed with confusion and slightly taken aback at her bluntness.

"I assume that is where you were this morning?"

"No! I was not!" I replied, shaking my head roughly.

"Boring. But were you with him?"

"Yeah, I gave him a lift to school. No, I didn't do anything to, or with him."

"Oh my god Lucy! You're *so* boring!"

"Thanks!"

Ignoring my offended tone, she continued.

"How do you even *survive* within school? Seriously, guys are everything."

I frowned, raising one eyebrow.

"Oh really?"

"Yes." She replied, definitively.

"Okay then Alice, whatever you say."

I knew that there was no use fighting with her, because she was just one of *those* girls.

Her look suddenly became one of concern, and her voice lowered an octave from her excited screeching.

"But what's wrong?"

"Nothing." I replied, not meeting her eyes.

"There obviously is Lucy. C'mon, out with it." She lightly bumped my shoulder. "We're best friends girl, and we have been for years. Have I not earned the right to be someone you trust?"

I didn't reply for a minute as I thought about how she had been my only friend for the past couple of years. I realised just how much I *did* trust her.

I was going to tell her.

"Alice…" I started. "What I'm about to tell you, you cannot tell a single other person. Do you understand?"

"Colour me intrigued." She replied, nodding.

"It's about Helena."

She frowned, obviously not having expected that response. "Helena?"

"Yes, my sister."

"Oh yeah, Helena."

I was slightly hurt that she hadn't remembered her, but I ignored the growing sense of discomfort in my stomach and carried on telling my story.

"She's alive."

"Didn't you say she died?" Her frown was still present.

"Yeah."

"Lucy, what are you on about? First you're bring up your dead sister, now apparently she's alive. What kind of stuff have you been smoking?"

The uncomfortable sensation in the pit of my gut increased in size as I sensed something was wrong. In hindsight, I really should have paid attention to it.

"Nothing. Alice, stop it. This is serious."

"Okay, serious. Go on."

Eyeing her with slight suspicion, I continued.

Taking a deep breath, I said "She's a Vampire."

Alice began laughing "What? You've completely lost it, girl."

"I'm serious!"

"Yeah, and I'm a witch." She replied, mocking me and wiggling her fingers, imitating casting a spell.

Dropping her hands, she just looked at me.

"You're a mess. I know that yesterday was 'the day', but you've survived the past, what, three years? I thought you wouldn't lose it this long after they died."

"Alice, what the hell is wrong with you? I am telling you something that is extremely important, and you're mocking me."

"What's wrong with me?! Lucy! Vampires don't exist!" She exclaimed.

"I'm sorry, but unlike your compassion or sympathy, they do. Lucien is one."

She let out a long sigh.

"Right. I'm going to humour you and go along with this. Okay, Lucien's a Vampire. How does he go out in the sun?"

I frowned, realising that I didn't actually have a response to that question.

"Why is his skin not really pale? Why doesn't he, you know, have those really long, sharp things coming from his mouth?"

She placed both of her index fingers at her canines, imitating a pair of fangs.

"That I can answer you – He does have fangs, and really black eyes too. You just can't see them unless he turns into his Vampire form."

"Oh, how convenient."

"I'm serious!"

"How much evidence do you have?"

I shook my head, disbelievingly "None, but the fact that I am telling you this proves that I have seen it!"

"No Lucy. If you *did* see a Vampire, it was a hallucination, nothing more."

"Why don't you believe me?!" I exploded.

"Because Vampires aren't real!" She shouted back.

"Lucy? Is everything okay up there?" My mum shouted up the stairs.

"Yeah we're fine, sorry." I yelled back. "Keep your voice down, Alice. Mum doesn't know."

"What, doesn't know that you're a psycho?"

"I'm telling you the truth." I stated bluntly.

"No you're not."

"Alice, I'm not having this argument with you again. Just forget I ever said anything, and don't tell anyone, okay?"

"Fine."

"Good."

There was a slight awkward silence between the two of us, before Alice shot a question at me.

"So, why'd you leave school early? You don't look ill."

"I couldn't focus on lessons as I'm seeing Helena tonight."

"Oh my GOD, Lucy!"

"Okay whatever, shut up. You asked a question, I answered it. Now are you just going to go on firing questions at me, or are you actually going to be nice?"

"I am being nice!"

Before I could respond, I got a text from Lucien:

*Hey Lucy, Elaine is outside the door. Tell your mum that she is one of Isaac's friends – She will explain the rest.*

*Hope you're doing alright. See you later.*

I frowned and quickly responded with:

*Elaine? Who's that?*

He immediately replied with:

*One of us, she will explain everything to you. Have fun ;)*

I frowned, but didn't respond.

'Have fun'? What was that supposed to mean?

That winking face was also very suspicious...

I shook my head and turned my attention to Alice.

"Someone is here. I'll be back in a minute." I informed her shortly, before exiting the room.


(Alice)

Good. Now she's gone, I can turn this awful stuff off.

What even was it? The screaming guitars were disgusting and what were those stupid, thudding, weird things?

I shot a look of extreme distaste at the phone, then returned to my seated position on the bed, pulling my own out of my pocket.

Oh! I had a text from Harry!

*Hey babe. That freak wasn't in class today. You know what's going on?*

I smiled at his message and immediately replied.

*Yeah, I know. She left early. She isn't just weird—Now, she's a complete psycho! You know that new guy? Lucien? She thinks he's a VAMPIRE!*

I knew that Harry wasn't one for texting back immediately, so I replaced my phone in my pocket and stood up.

I looked at a large, framed poster on Lucy's wall of five guys, all covered in black leather and tattoos.

"Ugh, who even are they?" I muttered.

I read the words 'Your Last Goodbye' written across the top of the poster.

"Of course."

I shook my head in discontent at the small group.

"I have no idea what she sees in these guys. Leather? Really? No."

I heard the beautiful, high pitched tone of Jake Smithy, joined by an acoustic guitar, coming from my pocket and I jumped in excitement.

I quickly pulled out my phone and was slightly reluctant to end the song, but it was Harry – I had to pick up.

"Hey babe!"

I was quiet for a minute as I listened to what he was saying.

"Yeah! I know right! Vampires... again. Like from ages ago!"

"Of course she wanted me to keep it a secret, just like before, and just like before, we're going to tell everyone. People really take well to the Vampire stuff."

He laughed in response, but then said that he had to go. "Oh, okay. Talk to you later, love you!"

He hung up and I walked back over to sit on Lucy's bed, ready to text Nicole and start up yet another wave of annoyance and torment for Lucy. This was entertaining.


(Lucy)

"Lucy? Are you expecting anyone?" My mother asked as I descended the stairs, walking out of the living room and leaning against the doorframe.

"Yeah, Isaac's friend is coming over - You know, because we are going to London tonight."

"Oh yeah, of course. If you need me, I'll be in the kitchen."

"Alright, thanks."

She had been surprisingly co-operative when Isaac had hypnotised her, hours before, and she seemed extremely supportive of my trip to London.

I slowly walked up to the front door and eyed it with suspicion for a moment, before turning the handle.

I had no idea what to expect when I swung the door open.

Would she be old or young?

Formal, or as chatty as Lucien?

I had no idea who I would be confronted with, but the woman that greeted me was certainly *not* what I had expected.

"Lucy! Darling! Oh you look *just* like your sister! Oh my gosh. What a lovely house! Are you going to invite me in?"

"Uh, hi. Elaine?"

She nodded excitedly, her short, dark, tight curls bouncing like springs.

48

"Yes, that's me! I guess Lucien didn't really explain who I was. Oh that is so like him – He does get a good laugh out of surprising people!"

I smiled politely and opened my mouth to say something. But apparently it seemed as though she wasn't going to let me get a word in edgeways.

"But yes, please invite me in. I believe I have some news that will be very enjoyable for you! Oh this is wonderful!"

"Yeah, of course. Come in."

"Oh thank you!" She replied, almost bouncing across the threshold.

"What a wonderful home! Oh this is very pretty. I love the colour scheme!"

"That'll be my mother – She likes decorating."

She clapped her hands in excitement. "Oh how brilliant, I can't wait to meet her! Helena has told me so much. I can tell that she is a woman with impeccable taste! I'm sure we will get on just fine!"

I escorted Elaine into the living room and walked into the kitchen that was in the adjoining room.

My mother turned her head when I entered and smiled at me.

I quickly and quietly closed the door, and all I could utter was "wow."

She raised an eyebrow expectantly.

"She's... eccentric."

"That sounds fun?"

"She's lovely, but yeah. Eccentric."

"Mhmm." My mother replied, turning back to cutting up the vegetables for dinner.

"Do you want to meet her? She likes how you've decorated the hall."

I heard her chuckle but she did not turn around.

"I'll be okay, thanks Lucy."

"Huh?" This was very unlike her as she was normally very protective and she also enjoyed meeting new people.

"It's just been a long day."

"Um. Okay. I'm going to go and talk to her... I'll see you later."

I exited the kitchen feeling extremely confused and I tried to dismiss the growing feeling of discomfort in my stomach that had begun with Alice's cold opinion on Helena.

Something was wrong and I knew it, but at that point I had too many things on my mind to be concerned by my natural instincts.

"Is everything okay Lucy? You look a bit shaken?" Elaine asked me, rising immediately from where she had seated herself on the crimson sofa, wearing a look of concern.

"I'm alright. So what is this 'amazing news'?"

She giggled and held a hand to her mouth.

"Oh you'll see! Can we go upstairs? I can tell you have a friend here, so I don't want to leave her out. I'm sure she will be extremely excited for you!"

"Sure." To tell the truth, I had almost completely forgotten about Alice. As I led Elaine upstairs, it dawned on me that telling Alice about Vampires may have been an extremely bad decision as, knowing her, I *knew* that she would, subtly or not, bring up our previous conversation. Elaine would *not* be happy about it, judging by the fact that she was in the same group as Isaac and Lucien. Lucien had made it blatantly clear that no-one else was to know about the fact that he was a Vampire...

I groaned inwardly as I opened my door, seeing Alice sprawled across my window seat, texting almost hungrily. I frowned with suspicion at her fast moving fingers, as she normally only acted that way when she received a new piece of 'gossip'.

Once again my natural instincts flared up, and once again I ignored them.

As if attempting to get my attention another way, a large wave of the familiar aching, burning pain shot up and down my spine.

I let out an audible indication of pain, drawing breath suddenly through my teeth, and this noise was what disrupted Alice from her animated digital conversation, causing her to immediately pocket her phone.

This was also out of character for her - she never just *stopped* texting someone.

"Lucy, hey!" She shot me a wide smile, but she also seemed slightly nervous at my entrance.

Within seconds that look had disintegrated, and she stood up when Elaine entered.

"Hi! You're Lucy's friend?" Elaine asked before raising an eyebrow questioningly at me, having seen Alice's bleach blonde hair and bright pink clothes.

I dismissed it immediately with a slight shake of my head, and she shrugged lightly, turning her attention back to Alice.

"Yeah, I'm Alice. Who are you?"

"I'm Elaine, Isaac - uh. Mr. Carter's friend."

Alice scowled "Alright... What's a teacher's friend doing here, Luc?"

I turned to Elaine for an answer, as I honestly had no clue.

"Well Alice, it's wonderful to meet you-"

I realised that Elaine seemed more controlled around Alice. It appeared that she only acted as excited as she did around people she knew. Then again, she had been eyeing Alice with extreme caution ever since she had entered the room.

"Isaac has informed me that he hasn't actually told Lucy where she is going in London yet."

I frowned. Was Elaine really going to tell a *human*, whom she had never met, about tonight's plans? Did that mean I okay in telling Alice about Helena?

"Well. Lucy?" Her eyes quickly flashed to my wall, and I followed her gaze, noting her mischievous smile.

All my attention became focussed on her as I saw that she had looked at my framed poster of 'Your Last Goodbye'.

Her smile only widened and I almost felt the excitement radiating off her.

"You're going on music trip."

"Oh." I felt myself become disappointed, but what confused me was the fact that Elaine's face still held a look of extreme giddiness.

"Oh did I fail to add? When I say 'music trip', I mean 'close observation' of a particular band, with back stage access, and a full meet and greet with the members."

I eyed her with suspicion, refusing to believe what I thought she was hinting at.

No. It wasn't possible.

"Look at me, missing out vital pieces of information! I'm not sure, but I think you'll enjoy this trip Lucy."

Her eyes then went to my shirt. Looking down, I saw that it was the shirt I had bought at 'Your Last Goodbye's concert, five months previous.

No.

Still, I disallowed myself to believe what she was almost spelling out for me.

"I mean, you seem to be a big fan of them. But I'm not sure. You're going to have to tell me Lucy... You like rock bands don't you? You enjoy loud music? You remember very clearly your meeting with James?"

Even though I had known what she was suggesting all along, my mouth hung open in pure shock and amazement.

"You don't mean..."

"Oh what? Them?" She pointed a perfectly manicured finger to the large poster of all five members.

"Oh yeah. You're not just going to say 'hi' this time. You're spending a full weekend with them. You'll be going to their concert this evening and you will be staying at a five star hotel. Then you're going to spend the full weekend doing whatever rock band members do."

I felt faint and I had to lower myself into my desk chair to keep standing.

"Am I missing something?" Alice asked, still sitting on the window seat.

In my extreme moment of happiness, I had forgotten about Alice, again.

Knowing that I was going to be unable to respond, Elaine turned her attention to the blonde haired girl who was sat, arms crossed, with a look of confusion on her face.

"Lucy's favourite band, 'Your Last Goodbye' have offered to let us have a look at their inside lives for Lucy's music project. Both she and Lucien have been chosen for this wonderful opportunity."

"Oh." She responded, seemingly bored by the conversation.

Elaine looked taken aback. "'Oh'? I thought you'd know about Lucy's admiration of them?" She addressed her, questioningly, indicating to my shirt with her thumb.

Alice rolled her eyes "Of course I know about her weird obsession. As you can possibly tell, I'm more of a pop girl."

"Either way, shouldn't you be a little happy for her?"

"Don't see why. I mean how does it affect me?"

Alice's obvious lack of interest in the conversation shook me from my moment of happiness and I frowned at her. Why was she acting so cold today?

"Lucy." Elaine said sharply. "Why don't you go downstairs and tell your mother this *brilliant* news." It was a command more than a suggestion, and for a moment, due to her sudden change from a chatty and happy exterior to an extremely judging, perhaps cold one, I was concerned for Alice's safety. Elaine seemed very protective over me for some reason. She had also put more emphasis on the word 'brilliant' to make Alice's immediate dismissal not seem as painful for me, and to remind me that it was okay to have at least a minute of excitement.

I nodded and left the room, descending the stairs to tell my mother what had just happened. Last time we were in London and we went to one of their concerts, she seemed really happy. Maybe this piece of news would raise her from her obvious sense of discomfort or displeasure of something else that had happened that day.

"Hey mum." I started as I entered the kitchen, hoping that her mood had changed.

"Hi sweetheart."

She *seemed* a little happier, but I wasn't about to pre-judge anything.

"Are you alright?"

"Yeah, I'm good. Sorry I didn't come out and meet your friend today."

"No, it's alright, she's upstairs talking with Alice at the moment I think."

"Alright."

"But-" I began, a large smile forming on my face. "I know Mr. Carter told you that we are going to London tonight..."

"Yeah, do you know what you're doing yet? All Isaac said was that you're doing something with school."

My grin became wider and I nodded excitedly.

"Yeah, Elaine told me!" I couldn't keep my happiness concealed any longer, and I burst out with "We are going to see 'Your Last Goodbye' perform *and* we are staying in a fancy hotel *and* we get to spend the full weekend with the band! For a research project for music!"

"Seriously? That's wonderful Lucy!" Although she seemed happy for me, her reaction almost seemed forced.

"Yeah, I'm really looking forward to it!" I jumped, clapping my hands, attempting to share my ecstatic feelings with her.

"You really should go back upstairs and get ready then Lucy. I know how much you like that band. You can borrow some of my make-up if you want." Her response seemed kind of like a dismissal, and frowning, I took the hint and slowly began walking back up the stairs.

That was when I heard it.

Half way up the stairs, Alice's poisonous words reached me and I sunk down against the wall in despair.

"No." I breathed.

"Oh, do you not know how she became so bullied? It was because of me. I told everyone her secret."

"No." I repeated, whimpering, placing my head in my hands as I heard the torturous words escaping her throat.

"Not her too. Please." I begged.

I had trusted yet another person who's only aim was to hurt me, use me, and leave me in the dirt, subjecting me to everyone else's mocking. *She* was the reason that my life had been hell. She had been one of the only people I had ever trusted...


(Elaine)

I didn't trust her.

Even if Lucy said that she was her friend, I did not trust her for a single moment.

Everything about her was wrong.

She was arrogant, cold, and completely the opposite of Lucy in every way.

Helena had told me such wonderful things about her sister, so why on earth was she even acquaintances with someone so judgemental and unsupportive as this girl in front of me.


I slowly walked towards her, and Alice eyed me with a look of suspicion, appearing to grow wary of me with each step I took.

"Alice." I said shortly, making eye contact with her.

"Yes?" She replied cautiously, unable to draw her eyes away from mine.

"Are you a good friend to Lucy?" I asked, enabling my powers of hypnosis.

"A good friend?" Her appearance of worry was immediately replaced by an arrogant one. "I don't think so, I mean does a good friend spread secrets? Like this one from today."

"What secret from today?" I asked, concerned that Lucy had divulged more information than she should have to *such* a trustworthy source.

"Oh, about Helena being a Vampire? She asked me really nicely not to say anything. But a Vampire... Really? She's turned into a complete psycho. She believes that Vampires are real. So what did I do? I texted everyone."

"You did *what?*" I seethed.

"Just like last time." She grinned maliciously. "Oh, do you not know how she became so bullied? It was because of me. I told everyone her secret. After her weird sister disappeared, she was really sad, so being the amazing person I am, I befriended her. I was failing at English anyway, so she was useful to me. But then I learned the interesting story that was Helena's Vampire related disappearance. Well, judging by how you act, I doubt you were popular as a child, so I'll explain the inner workings of popularity to you. You're only useful if you supply a constant flow of information. Alright?" She spoke to me as if educating a young child, and my annoyance and disgust for this creature grew by the second "So here was Lucy, a lonely, little, vulnerable girl with no friends, no attractive features, no boyfriend, and someone who had just lost two close members of her family." Her voice had taken on a mocking form of concern, and then quickly turned back to a bragging arrogance. "Then there's me: the most gorgeous, popular one of them all, dating Harry, the best footballer in the school and, I don't mean to brag, but probably the best in bed out of all the guys. In what world would Lucy and I *ever* cross paths? In what reality would we *ever* be friends. Unless I wanted something from her. She supplied me with a fresh story, something to put to use."

"You are a disgusting piece of work." I hissed at her through clenched teeth, shaking my head.

"Oh I pride myself on getting responses like that. When you've been in the game as long as I have, you learn a thing or two about being manipulative." She gave me a sly grin. "So thanks to our little Lucy's loose mouth, Helena's secret is out."

"No. It's not. I am going to remove every memory of you even being here today."

Alice's sly look changed to one of confusion, and her eyebrows furrowed.

"Because you know what Alice? Vampires *do* exist. You're facing one."

Her eyes became wide. "That isn't possible."

"Oh really?" I smiled, and as I opened my mouth my fangs elongated out from my canines, and I felt my vision acquire a slightly dark tinge.

"YOU BITCH!" Lucy burst through the door, almost shattering it off its hinges, a burning fire in her eyes as she ran straight for Alice.


(Lucy)

I grabbed her by her beloved blonde hair and pulled her from her seated position, slamming her to the floor, shouting roughly into her face.

"HOW COULD YOU?!!" I screamed, pulling my fist back and repeatedly striking her.

After a few seconds, I saw blood pouring from her nose, but this dangerous frenzy that she had forced me into made me want nothing more than to tear her limb from pathetic limb.

"I TRUSED YOU!" I shrieked, continuing my assault, slapping at her, tearing at her hair, but before I could do any more damage, I felt a pair of extremely strong hands lift me off Alice's thrashing form.

The second Elaine had removed me from my target, Alice sat upright, smiling, ignoring the split in her lip and the blood flowing freely from her nose.

"Is that all you've got little girl? Do you really have no more anger, no more hatred for me? You know I ruined your life right? I turned everyone against you."

Elaine held me firmly in place so no matter how much I struggled against her grasp, I was unable to escape.

"When your stupid sister went missing, and your pathetic father got himself killed–"

A new kind of rage coursed through my veins and I felt my vision go hazy as I screamed and arched my back against Elaine, forcing my feet off the ground and straight into Alice's stomach, throwing her back onto the floor.

"I'M GOING TO BLOODY KILL YOU, YOU HEARTLESS BITCH!"

"Was that meant to hurt?" Alice asked, indicating to her stomach, but I could tell by her slight breathlessness, and how she was stood, that I had in fact caused her a decent amount of pain.

This fact brought me a small amount of satisfaction, but it was quenched by the blinding desire to draw more blood and force more pain through her system.

"Enough of this." Elaine seethed, holding me tighter.

I felt the small hairs on the back of my neck stand on end as she made eye contact with Alice.

"Shut the hell up and go home. You don't remember anything about Vampires from today."

Alice slyly grabbed her bag and crossed the carpet, giving me a little mocking wave as she left the room.

# CHAPTER FOUR

I thrashed hard against Elaine, determined to free myself and chase after Alice, throwing her down the stairs or causing her a similar degree of pain.

She had awoken something within me that had been dormant for the past three years:

The last time I had felt like this, was the day I found out that both my father and Helena had 'died'.

At first I was lost in despair, crying myself to sleep throughout the day, refusing to leave my room.

But then the anger came:

The all encompassing rage that flooded my system, boiled my blood and turned my mind to fire.

The room had been filled with a suffocating, inky darkness and I had been sat with my back against the base of my bed when I felt it. I was no longer able to cry and at first I felt withdrawn from the world, like an empty shell of my former body, but within that emptiness, a new host took its place:

Something with a heart of fire and the mind of a killer.

My eyes had then come back into focus but this newfound dark strength within me filled me with adrenaline, and I knew that I needed to get out of the house.

I exited the building and ran hard, the dark shadows of the night flying past me, and the darkness that had once unnerved me, now felt like home. That evening, not a single creature stirred and even the moon did not turn its head, seemingly fearful of my terrifying, inhuman rage.

What resided within me at that moment, I would never be able to truly describe, but all I knew was that I was extremely dangerous and if anyone was to utter a single word to me, I would have broken their bones without blinking. That night I was a hunter, looking for something to kill.


That was exactly how I felt right now.

The second Alice had mentioned my father was when the darkness had taken hold of me once again. That moment was when the animalistic rage had gripped my soul and forced me into a state of bloodlust.

My mother had never been aware of what happened to me that night, and she still remained in the dark with the whole subject.

Or perhaps it was the light.

She remained in a beautiful, naive light, and I had been banished to a tormenting darkness that threatened to rear its ugly head at any moment, catching me off guard, making me a dangerous threat to everyone.

I had contemplated running away.

I had contemplated going to a therapist, claiming insanity, and forcing them to lock me away in a padded cell. But there was only one thing that had stopped me from doing that when I returned home, and it was *them*.

The members of 'Your Last Goodbye'.

The fast paced, pounding drum beats that mirrored my racing heart.

The shrieking, screaming guitars that banished the torturous howls from my mind.

Then there was his voice.

The sounds and the words that had saved me.

The first three songs had been very heavy ones, filled with a loud, aggressive combination of instruments, letting me come to terms with my newfound rage. But the one that followed, 'The Eyes to the Soul' had been the soothing song that had pulled me back from the edge.

Beginning with a slow, beautiful piano, the notes had entered mind, soothing every inch of my body and calming my heartbeat. Finally, it let me breathe freely, causing me to not feel as though everything within me was on fire.


This band had saved me from travelling down an extremely dark path, but it was not I who had found them.

It had been Helena.

Even from beyond the grave -or so I thought- she was protecting me, this time, from myself.


That cursed night, when I returned home, I was alone. My mother had decided to go to a restaurant with a friend in an attempt to cheer her up from the loss of her husband and daughter, so I was by myself –Which was good, because the second I entered my room, I began tearing everything apart.

I had let out numerous, pained howls, unable to control the anger within me as I threw books, my chair, clothes and an array of many other things at the four walls that had once held happy memories for me.

As I tore the drawer from my desk off its hinges, I saw something that was nestled within it that stopped me in my tracks.

My sister's mp3 player.

My mind flashed back to the hours we had spent dancing around my room, singing into hairbrushes and laughing the day away. That momentary break in my destructive phase was all I needed.

The whole world seemed to stop, an empty silence filling my mind as I reached a shaking hand down to the small, red device. The second my skin had made contact with the cool metal, I took an intake of breath, closing my eyes as more memories flashed back to me: Her smile and the sound of her laugh.

Opening my eyes, I turned the device on and I was met by a photograph of both Helena and myself.

I lost myself for a moment in the photograph, staring at her smiling face, recalling the hot summer evening on which that photograph was taken. We were sat around a bonfire with both our parents, roasting marshmallows and laughing at my father's foul attempts at playing classical guitar and singing.

A small smile crossed my face, accompanied by a single tear that slowly rolled down my cheek and onto the floor.

"Helena." I had breathed, reaching up to trace her face with my thumb.

Then the screen faded to black and I was once again alone.

I felt it. The fiery rage. I felt it slowly clawing its way back to me. I could see flashes of it out of the corner of my eye:

A dark, deadly creature, stalking me, hiding just out of clear sight.

That was the first time I had seen it; the darkness in my peripheral vision; the disease that seemed to feed on my sadness, and once it had had its fill, it would possess my mind with a deadly rage that would destroy anything its path.

That was the first time I had ever thought that it wasn't me. Every day since, I had simply dismissed it as a reflection of my imagination running away with itself.

That was the only day I had ever been right about the torturous creature.

Sure enough, the entity got its desire and possessed my soul once again.

Racing across the room, I had tossed my pillows and blanket from my bed. I had torn the sheet covering my mattress free, and as I was about to throw the thick, springy base from the wooden frame, I accidentally tapped the power button for the mp3 player and once again the pain subsided, the light of the screen forcing my darkness to cower into a corner.

I had slowly lowered myself onto the bare mattress, and with a shaking hand, I unlocked the device, scrolling through her music until I came to the band 'Your Last Goodbye'.

Looking back, perhaps I saw their name fitting: My last goodbye to both my father and Helena. My attempt to let them, and the pain, go.

The first song had been a loud one, and I jumped slightly as I was greeted by a thudding drum beat. But the second the vocalist had begun singing, I felt my eyes close and I laid sideways on the bed, feeling the battle in my mind between the terrifying darkness, and the familiar, safe voice of James.

That was the first night they had saved me.


I opened my eyes and I found that I was laid on my bed. Rolling slowly sideways, I saw Elaine sat on my wooden chair, her back to my desk, smiling sadly at me.

"Hey." She said, giving me a comforting look.

From how she was acting, I *knew* what she had done – She had read my dream.

"You saw that, didn't you?" I asked for clarification.

She nodded slowly. "Yes, I did."

I raised myself up into a sitting position, leaning against my headboard, and I took a sharp intake of breath through my teeth as I felt the stabbing pain ricochet up my spine.

Elaine frowned at me, a concerned look on her face.

"What's wrong?"

"Nothing." I shook my head. "It just feels like something is sat on my back, stabbing me every few minutes."

Her frown remained unmoving.

"How long has this been happening?"

"Well, my back has been aching for ages, but it has only become painful recently."

"Hm." She responded shortly, keeping her gaze on me.

In the blink of an eye, her mood changed.

"Okay. So you've had your rant. You've had your nostalgia moment regarding Helena. Now let's get you ready for a weekend you will never forget." Although she gave me a wide smile, I saw something in her eyes that still held a feeling of confusion and concern for me.

Not having the energy to push the matter further, I smiled back at her, surrendering to her excitement.

"Alright. What do you mean 'get ready'?"

I saw the concern fade from her eyes and I believed that our previous discussion had well and truly been put on the backburner, her full attention having been given to the situation at hand.

She giggled and clapped excitedly, almost returning to the woman I had met at the beginning of the evening.

"Wait here!" She shot up from her chair and raced out of the room, her image becoming a blur.

I frowned after her as I actually had no idea what she meant by 'getting me ready' for this evening. Was she going to play dress up or something? I looked down at my clothes and saw that I wasn't exactly dressed in the appropriate attire for a rock concert.

A smile spread across my face as I remembered the 'cover story' for the weekend. I became confused though, as I wasn't sure if I was *actually* going to meet them again, or if that had just been a false story to hide the fact that I would be seeing Helena.

A few moments later, Elaine ran back into my room with a hefty, leather suitcase.

"What's in *that?*" I asked.

She grinned. "It's to 'get you ready' for this weekend!"

"That's a point, Elaine, am I really meeting them or did you just say that to keep blondie off the trail?"

I literally could not say her name, for fear of it bringing back a spark of anger, so I had simply replaced it with 'blondie'.

"Oh, of course you're still meeting them. Helena is seeing us there. Also, there's a reason that you won't have heard that the band is touring. It's because they're not: This is a private showing and there will only be a small  group of people in the audience." She smiled to herself, as if enjoying a personal joke.

"That's amazing." I muttered.

"Only the best for the reunion between you and Helena."

She smiled at me for a moment before adding "She's missed you. She really has."

"Trust me, it has been mutual." I responded. "At least she knew that I was still alive."

"Yes, and it tortured her. The fact that you were alive and she couldn't contact you or your mother, to tell you she was okay, tore her apart inside. You've grieved her death. She's grieved your life."

I froze. I had never thought about it like that, but now that I had, I felt so much sympathy for her. She must have felt so alone. As far as I was aware, she was *gone* and not coming back. But she kept living every day, wondering if we would ever meet again because there *was* a chance of a reunion between us. It must have killed her waiting for it.

"But let's not get upset! There's nothing to be sad about anymore. She's alive and you're going to see her. You're seeing your favourite band performing and then you're going to spend a full weekend with them. Seriously Lucy, drop any negativity right now and let's get you ready. Now, any music preferences?"

I grinned and nodded, walking to my phone and within seconds the song 'Hell's Angel' began playing. I trotted over to my desk and placed my phone onto the docking station, increasing the volume. Less than a second later, I was greeted by James's familiar, deep voice, the heavy, constant drum beat from Chris, Ben's resounding bass and Josh and Damian's shrieking electric guitars.

Elaine grinned "You really do like this band, don't you?" Her face still held a look that gave the impression that she knew something I didn't.

"Yeah, definitely. You read my 'dream', or whatever it was, so you know just how much power they actually have over me."

"Interesting." She muttered, the smile not leaving her face.

"Okay!" She exclaimed, indicating to the leather case in her hand. "These are yours. Helena said that you would like leather." She knelt down and placed it on the floor, preparing to open it, but quickly shot up, as if remembering something.

"Oh! Before I let you see inside, I have something else for you." She reached an elegant hand into the inside pocket of her black jacket, procuring a white envelope with my name written on the front of it.

The second I saw my name written on the pale material, I froze.

It was Helena's handwriting.

I looked between Elaine and the envelope, and back again.

Even though I was sure that Helena's existence wasn't a lie, this past day the thought had momentarily entered my mind on numerous occasions. Part of my mind admitted that this situation appeared entirely insane: My twin sister *wasn't* dead; she had just simply been turned into a Vampire... Which just happened to be a mythological creature that *shouldn't* even exist.

But then I had seen Lucien transform into a Vampire, and in that moment, I had been almost one hundred percent sure that my sister was alive.

Seeing this letter reminded me of the few times I had questioned her existence, but now that I saw her handwriting, any suspicion had been quenched and destroyed.

Now it was certain: My sister was alive.

I slowly took the letter from Elaine, treating it as though it was a piece of gossamer, able to break apart in my hands at any moment.

A small frown crossed my features as I felt that the envelope was weighted – There was something inside it, other than a piece of paper.

Both confused and curious, I opened the delicate envelope, and as I pulled the letter out and slowly opened it, a silver necklace fell out onto my hand.

Upon closer inspection, I recognised it immediately.

It was Helena's necklace. Reaching up to my neck, I found my own, identical to the one resting in the palm of my hand.

Looking down, I saw the small, circular, onyx stone, framed by an extremely thin edging of silver. This was definitely hers. For our fifteenth birthday, we had walked past a jewellery store with our parents and the pair of necklaces had immediately caught both of our attentions.

Noticing our immense interest, my father had decided to buy us one each. It turned out that the necklaces were both uniquely crafted, the symbol of a triskelion engraved into them. This was a Celtic symbol, also known as the 'spiral of life' and this beautiful shape was made up of three half curls, all pointing in an anticlockwise direction. It represented the cycle of life, death, and rebirth.

I smiled at the bitter irony of the symbol and also our naivety at the point of buying the jewellery – We merely thought that they were 'pretty'. We could never have guessed at the extent to which the symbol applied to Helena: Her birth, her death, and then her re–birth into a Vampire.

Curling my fingers around the necklace, I turned my attention to the letter.

*Dear Lucy,*

*I hope this letter finds you in good health–*

*Nope, I can't do it! I'm not going to be posh, calm, or collected about this.*

*I'M ALIVE LUC!*

*I have been wanting to tell you this for the past three years, but I couldn't. I have missed you so much it hurts.*

*Isaac has been telling me that ever since my 'disappearance', you have been researching Vampires, and due to this everyone in school turned on you.*

*Trust me, if I could have come back, Harry would have been my first target. It has infuriated me knowing that you were being hurt and tormented, so much so that I physically got into a fight with someone about leaving the house and coming to help you.*

*Unfortunately I picked a fight with an elder, which didn't end well. But whatever, I'm completely fine and tonight is the night Lucy, after all these years...*

*We get to see each other again.*

*If you haven't heard, we are meeting at a YLG concert! Apparently since I came here, you turned into a bit of a fan. Good on ya' girl!*


I chuckled, remembering her love for the band, which some may have called a slight obsession.

*I love you so much Lucy, it has hurt like hell being away from you, but i'm going to round up this letter now.*

*I'll see you tonight.*

*Love,*
*Helena*

At the very bottom of the page, another message was written:

*I know all of this is almost impossible to believe, but it is true. I am alive. To prove it to you, accompanied with this letter is my necklace. I have not taken it off since our fifteenth birthday, when you fastened it around my neck, but I had to send you something to prove to you that this was true. Please bring it with you when you come tonight. Also, it's funny how the symbol on the back basically relates to me. Bye Luc! Enjoy the clothes!*

I closed my hand tighter around the silver, focussing on the solid *proof* of her existence, holding it close to me.

Breaking the moment of silence, Elaine spoke up "See? She is alive. This is actually happening Lucy."

"Yeah. I know that now."

"Good. Now let's talk appearances. I know you love James, I can tell by the shrine." She pointed to the large, framed poster on the wall.

"It's not a shrine-" I attempted to interject, but she cut me off.

"You're a fangirl and he is physically attractive. It's a shrine. Anyway, so because you obviously love James, you're going to want to look your very best."

"Helena has told you everything about me, hasn't she?"

"Yep. She personally picked the clothes out for you too. So, from my chats with Helena, apparently you're wanting to basically look like a 'rocker-chick', yes?"

I nodded. "That sounds about right."

"Brilliant. Here's the suitcase, so choose what you want to wear tonight. Then I can get on with your make-up and hair. I'll be up in about ten minutes, I'm just going to go and call Isaac to sort things out for tonight. Have fun!"

"See you later." I called after her, as she almost skipped out of the room, closing the door behind her.

I turned my attention to the large leather suitcase situated in front of me and eyed it with curiosity.

I wondered what type of clothing waited for me inside, but judging by my clue being 'leather', I could have a pretty good guess.

Kneeling down in front of it, I saw that there was a three digit code that had to be entered to open it. I was about to call Elaine, but a thought came into my mind, causing me to smile. "Okay, this is definitely Helena's doing if this works."

I slowly turned each number to six, and sure enough it opened.

"Wow. Number of the devil. Original." I muttered sarcastically, a smile still on my face as I shook my head.

What waited for me inside wasn't *exactly* what I had expected. First of all, it wasn't only clothes that were contained within this suitcase. The word 'trunk' was probably a better word for this large object.

It was sectioned out into three parts:

Clothes.

Shoes.

Jewellery.

I wasn't what a lot of people would call a 'girly girl', so I wasn't completely obsessed with clothes. But I had to admit that this was impressive and a grin crossed my face in excitement of my gifts.


After five minutes of sifting through the beautiful garments and accessories, I selected a pair of black, lace up combat boots, a thin choker necklace, a pair of dark fitted jeans, a matching tank top with the band's logo on and finally, I chose a perfectly tailored leather biker jacket, adorned with studs on the lapels.

I quickly got changed, pulling the new clothes over my skin and discarding the original ones on my window seat. I walked over to the side of my desk and looked in my full body mirror, placing my hands on my jacket lapels. I was taken aback by just *how* perfectly the clothes fitted me and for once, I actually felt happy about my appearance. I hadn't really cared about how other people judged me, because since Helena's disappearance I had grown a thick skin anyway, but I hadn't ever been completely happy with how I looked. I also felt as though the clothes that I had chosen actually let me be myself. Already, I felt as though as I was fitting into Helena's new world. Even though I knew that this was only a simple visit to see her and that I wouldn't be staying, it still made me feel that I belonged with her.

Whilst moving to see my appearance at a different angle, my eyes caught the reflection of the large poster which held the clear image of all five men from 'Your Last Goodbye', and I turned to face it.

I sighed as I looked over their faces, remembering all of the issues that this band had helped me through;  all the sleepless nights; the nightmares that pushed their way into any moments of rest that came to me; both my father's and Helena's passing, and the days that followed.

Now, most of those experiences that had haunted me for the past three years had finally come to pass, and at every turn that band had been there. The members of 'Your Last Goodbye', had kept me alive, given me a reason to live, and made me want to cling to the brilliant things in life: My mother, my boyfriend of the time, and my only friend... Alice.

I suddenly froze, seeing a black flicker in the corner of my left eye. The creature that had been haunting me had awoken, ready to force itself into my mind and corrupt my thought processes once again.

Suddenly a loud, screeching guitar cut through the air, and it banished the monstrosity back to its origin, the next song having begun playing.


Elaine trotted back into the room, beaming at me.

"You look gorgeous Lucy, and *perfect* for this evening's entertainment! I knew Helena had a good eye for clothes, as do you my dear, for selecting them. Now, if you don't mind, please do not move from this seat for the next hour." She smiled at me, moving my chair from my desk and sitting it in front of my mirror. "You're about to become a badass rocker chick that will make even James blush." She chuckled at my red cheeks as I sat down.


*An hour later*

"Perfect!" Elaine exclaimed, standing back from me and admiring her work.

I had to hand it to her – my hair looked amazing and my make-up caused me look as though I belonged even more in the 'rocker-chick' category that Elaine kept referring to.

"It's brilliant, thank you."

She batted her hand in a dismissive fashion, but I could tell that she was still pleased I approved of my appearance. "I've had a lot of experience. Besides, I can only enhance beauty that already exists. Either way, I bet James will love it!"

Just as I opened my mouth to say something, I heard the doorbell ring and Elaine said "That's Lucien with the car, are you ready to leave?"

My heart rate suddenly increased.

Elaine obviously sensed this and grinned at me "Yeah Lucy, it is happening."

I nodded, unable to form any words as I stared at my reflection, trying to calm my racing heart and control my excitement, but failing immensely.

After taking a deep breath and closing my eyes, I stood up from my chair, collected my phone, my headphones and Helena's necklace, gripping it tightly.

I then stood in front of Elaine, my right fist clenched around the silver chain. "I'm ready." I muttered before she smiled and I followed her out of the room.

Her words reverberated around my skull all the way down the stairs and out onto the concrete of the driveway.

*It is happening. It is happening. It is happening.*

It was almost a chant, a ritual in my mind that swirled, refusing to fade for even a fraction of a second from the forefront of my mind.

As if in a dazed state, I noticed my mother leant against the wall at the end of the driveway, waiting for me.

When I arrived, she turned and began walking towards me.

"I'm sorry that I was so dismissive and distant earlier, sweetheart."

She placed her arms around my torso, hugging me.

I returned the embrace, telling her that it was alright, and when I pulled back, I saw a strange smile etched onto her blood red lips: Something that was somewhere between a malicious excitement and a bored relief. It was a look that I had not once seen cross her face. It was as though she was looking *forward* to something happening, something that would free her. That brief, uneasy feeling once again flooded my system, and the words *it is happening* were suddenly spoken in a very aggressive, mocking, dangerous tone.

That was when my body forced me to not ignore the unnerving feeling anymore. I had an overwhelming sense of dread, my smile dropped, and my whole body felt suffocated with a feeling of terror of what the very near future held.

I was terrified of something. But I had no idea where that fear had stemmed from. It had been on my mind all day.

The pain in my back...

Alice's betrayal...

My mother's distant and strange emotions...

As individual, isolated incidents, they were just common, daily hassles. But combined? Something was going to happen. I couldn't pinpoint what exactly, and that was the thing that terrified me the most:

The fear of the unknown.

"Lucy?" Came a masculine call from the sleek black vehicle that was parked out on the road.

I slowly turned my head, the feeling of uneasiness still residing within me as I saw Lucien exiting the car.

"Are you coming?" He asked.

Nodding slightly, I tentatively took two steps towards the vehicle. Five minutes previously, seeing that car would have brought me a great deal of happiness, as it would have held the prospect of seeing Helena again, and also seeing the members of my favourite band.

But now, I had a terrible sense of dread that only grew with each step. My instincts were screaming at me to *not* get in that car. They were telling me to run away as fast and as hard as I could, and in that moment, I had half a mind to obey them, but something drove me on.

Something forced me to place one foot in front of the other.

Something forced me to get into the car behind Lucien, and to not once look back.

Even as we pulled away I did turn to wave goodbye to my mother.


Then again, if I had looked back to bid her farewell, I would have been even more scared. For within the eyes of the woman who leant against that stone wall, a bright, blood red flicker was seen...

# CHAPTER FIVE

I t is happening.
     *It is happening.*
*It is happening.*

Those three words reverberated around my skull, becoming even more aggressive with each syllable. The closer I arrived to my destination, the more terrified I became.

*Stop.* I commanded, mentally.

There was a brief pause, but then the words continued, even louder than before.

I closed my eyes, leaning back against the smooth leather of the seat.

*Please.* I begged.

My pleas -like always- were unanswered and ignored, so I did the only thing I knew how to do to stop the fear.

I opened my eyes and reached down into my front pocket, pulling my black headphones free.

Without saying a word, and ignoring -to the best of my ability- the demonic chant in my mind, I plugged the headphones into my phone. I selected a loud, aggressive song and then placed them in my ears.

I let out an audible sigh and Lucien turned to look to me, having previously been engaged in a conversation with Elaine.

I saw him mouth something but I was unable to hear him over my music, so I removed one headphone and asked him to repeat what he had said.

"I asked, are you alright? You look worried."

I nodded slightly.

"Yeah. I'm just... experiencing a different combination of emotions right now." I muttered.

It wasn't strictly a lie.

"Hmm. Okay." He eyed me with suspicion, knowing that something else was wrong, but he decided not to push me further.

I gave him a weak smile and then replaced my headphone, turning to look out of the window at the bright lights flashing by.

After a few moments of staring aimlessly out of the window, my eyes drifted to a close and I leant against the cool glass, the music flooding my mind. As always, the sound of James's voice had silenced my fears and calmed my racing heart.

With my newfound peace, my mind drifted to the thought of seeing him again.

Would he remember me?

I smiled sarcastically to myself.

Of course he wouldn't - I'm one in thousands of people who told him that he had saved them.

Because that is what he, and the other members of 'Your Last Goodbye' did: They saved people.

They gave people those moments of happiness and light that they so much desired and required to, in some cases, continue living.

Those five men saved lives. For that I would forever be in awe of them, and I would always thank them for being the support I needed to save me from the darkness which had threatened to engulf me.

I felt a small nudge against my arm and I opened my eyes to see Lucien smiling at me.

I removed my headphones and looked at him.

"What?" My voice sounded weak and I suddenly realised that I had fallen asleep.

"We're here. It is happening."

My face fell.

The second he said those three words, the voice in my mind immediately awoke – This time it was quiet, almost a whisper.

*It is happening.*

I realised that the voice wasn't that of a whisper, it was one of death.

Those three words were only uttered once, and then a silence fell over my mind.

But I was not relieved.

I was *petrified*.

The bodiless voice had not just decided to stop after sensing my distress: It had *warned* me and then fell silent, leaving me to witness the final hours of my life alone.

Now I was certain of it.

I was going to die that evening.

I had never been fearful of death. I had been confused more than scared. But in that moment, the fear that flooded my system at the unknown nature of my impending doom almost paralysed me. The familiar aching fire shot up and down my spine and I almost fainted, but I heard Lucien say.

"It's time. You're going to see Helena."

*Helena.*

With as much strength as I could muster, I once again pushed every single piece of fear to the back of my mind and immediately it tried to free itself, but with my newfound strength of seeing my sister again, I forced it back into the dark recesses of my soul.

Within that moment, a sense of urgency and excitement coursed through me, and I audibly muttered "Helena" before I shoved my phone into my pocket and grabbed my door handle, launching myself out of the vehicle.

I noticed that we had arrived at a large, gothic mansion, instead of an arena or concert venue, but I had no time to question where I was.

I raced up a flight of stone steps and threw myself at a set of double oak doors.

The second I entered the building, I could feel the fearful emotions screaming to be let back into the forefront of my mind, warning me of my surroundings. From my body's response, I guessed that everyone who surrounded me was a Vampire.

I pushed my way roughly through the crowd, scanning every face, searching for her.

Then time froze.

The large group of people that were gathered in the room appeared to drop away as she and I locked eyes.

It was her.

Her dark, straight hair fell perfectly around her shoulders and her whole face had taken on a look of inhuman beauty that I had never been before. But it was her eyes that caught my attention the most.

They were still her own, but I saw that they were haunted.

With every second that her gaze fell upon me, I almost *felt* her despair fall away.

"Helena..." I breathed.

With that word, I broke the silence between us and she launched herself across the room at me.

"Lucy!"

We both held each other hard and refused to let go.

I felt my tears fall but at that moment, I did not care.

Nothing else mattered.

No-one else mattered.

She was safe.

Helena was safe, and she was in my arms.

I hugged her tighter and we both started sobbing into each other's shoulders.

Still keeping her arms securely wrapped around me, Helena pulled back and looked at me, elated tears in her eyes.

"Lucy." Was all she could manage to say, but I nodded, responding with "I know. I'm here."

She nodded, more tears freeing themselves and falling down her cheeks.

She once again pulled me towards her.

"Hey, be careful." I chuckled gruffly, my voice distorted by my tears. "You're stronger than me now."

She pulled back and a joking, competitive look entered her eyes "I always was, sister."

I saw that even saying the word 'sister' brought her great happiness.

"Speaking of strength–" Helena cleared her throat, attempting to return her voice back to its normal tone, after having had so many tears make their way through her system "you're looking pretty badass in your leather." She then chuckled. "It seems you have passed over to the 'dark side'."

I smiled back, nodding. "It seems so. Well. I'm not a Vampire, so not completely."

"Ouch!" She responded, softly shoving me.

Just like that, we had resorted back to the way we were before; as if nothing had happened; as if no time at all had passed; as if I had not thought that she had been *dead* for three years.

"Anyway, I can't take all the credit; apparently these clothes were of your choosing?" I queried.

She nodded "Well, I heard that you were a big fan of 'Your Last Goodbye'." Just like the others, a knowing smile crossed her lips.

"What don't I know?" I asked her.

"Nothing. Nothing at all." She replied, keeping her eyes fixed on mine, that knowledgeable grin still residing on her face.

As I was about to question her further, a masculine voice resounded from behind me.

"I see you have met someone you know, Lucy."

I turned to face a tall, handsome man with short black hair and piercing blue eyes.

"Hey Marius." Helena beamed. "Lucy, this is Mr. Killoran, Lucien's dad."

Killoran.

That name...

I had heard that name so many times before...

Where the hell did I know it from?!

With my complete array of mixed emotions, it seemed as though my mind failed to remember anything.

"Hello Lucy. It is a pleasure to finally meet you."

"You too, I hope Helena hasn't told you too many stories about me."

He smiled, revealing a set of pearly white teeth. I noticed that he had larger and sharper canines than any of the other Vampires surrounding him. That was interesting. Even in human form, elders seemed to be slightly more animalistic in appearance.

I quenched the textbook side of my mind and my attention was drawn back to the moment at hand.

"On the contrary, miss Brown: You're all Helena has been talking about these past three years. We know everything about you." He spoke each word correctly, pronouncing each syllable perfectly as he fixed his eyes on me with an impenetrable gaze.

Those eyes...

I had seen those eyes...

I was interrupted in my thoughts as Lucien entered the room.

"Father, leave her alone. She's just got here and you're already freaking her out."

80

Lucien turned to me and Marius quickly said "Farewell." before walking back off into the crowd of people.

"Ignore him: He enjoys making people feel uncomfortable."

His eyes fell to Helena, and a warm look passed between the two of them. Not tearing his eyes away from hers, he said "I see you found Helena."

"Yeah, I couldn't be happier. Thank you so much Lucien."

Slowly, he pulled his gaze from hers and looked at me.

"It's my pleasure."

"But" Helena interjected, grabbing my arm. "I think it's time we made you *even* happier."

I frowned in confusion as she pulled me through the crowd of people, over to the opposite side of the room where a group of men were seated at a table.

Helena stood in front of me, blocking my line of vision and she suddenly said "Lucy. You said that you couldn't be happier, yes?"

"What are you up to..?"

"Answer the question!" She commanded excitedly, almost jumping.

"Okay. Yes, I did."

Her grin became wider. "Well. In the next five seconds, you're going to be ecstatic. Killoran, you've got a guest!" I had guessed that she was talking to Lucien, so I turned around to face him, a deep frown still etched on my face, but I saw that his gaze had fallen to someone behind me.

I followed his line of vision and saw that Helena had moved aside, and the man that had been sat behind her turned around to face me.

My body froze.

"No." I breathed.

My breath caught in my throat and for the second time that evening, the whole world seemed to freeze as a set of piercing blue eyes held me.

"Lucy." Helena began "Meet James Killoran, the lead singer of 'Your Last Goodbye' and the brother of Lucien."

My mouth fell open as James stood up and looked at me, a perfect smile spreading across his features.

"Lucy... That name... We've met before." I could tell by his eyes that he was joking: He knew *exactly* who I was.

Right now, I was a bewildered fan who had been caught extremely off guard.

All I could reply with was a weak nod and an even weaker "Y–yes."

He reached into his inside pocket, produced a folded up piece of paper, and held it up to me.

"Remember this?" He asked.

Was that? – No it couldn't be. He couldn't have kept it after all this time...

"*Dear James...*" His reading of my letter brought me out of my shocked reverie and forced words out of my mouth.

"You kept it?"

He looked at me over the top of the letter, raising an eyebrow.

"Of course I did. I always keep things of great importance to me."

I felt myself blushing crimson. Only minutes previously, I had believed that he wouldn't even recognise me when we met again, let alone say that something I had written was of *great importance* to him.

He shot me another smile before folding the sheet of paper back up and replacing it in his inside pocket, exactly like he had done all those months ago.

"So, I take it that this is a surprise?" Helena intercepted.

I turned to her mischievous, grinning face. "You *knew!*"

"Of course I knew, woman! I live here!"

"Hey, Ladies? Sorry to interrupt, but it's midnight. We have to go somewhere."

I turned back to James and I looked around him, realising that the men sat at the table were his fellow band members.

Of course I didn't want him to leave, but I couldn't do anything about it, so I turned my gaze back to Helena.

It was obvious that my face held a look of disappointment as she said "Oh don't look like that, Luc! Did you forget why you're here? You came to meet the band and see them perform... the party is only just beginning."

The second she finished speaking, a fast, steady drum beat resounded around the room and I slowly turned on my heel to see a lit stage in the centre of the back wall.

Suddenly, two guitars began playing a tune I knew all too well, and shortly after them, amazing deep lyrics followed:

> 'The fire and brimstone running through my veins,
> The pitch black smoke clouding your face,
> The scorching flames licking the walls of this cell,
> Welcome, my dear, to Hell.'

I ran across the room to the front of the stage as Josh began his guitar solo for 'Hell's Angel'.

James strode forward slightly, and he seemed to be moving with the drum beat, but within a second he had come down from the stage, grabbed me around the waist and hoisted me back up with him.

I heard a faint cheer from Helena as James released me slightly. The sound of Josh's guitar had also become quieter.

I looked around the room and I spied Lucien stood next to the guitar amp, having been the one to turn the volume down. He had a massive grin on his face.

"So! Everyone!" James started, his arm still around my waist.

Oh crap. He *wasn't* going to...

"We have a *very* special guest here today!"

*Oh no.*

He looked to me and winked.

I nearly fainted.

"This is a *very* special girl that you have all heard so much about from her brilliant sister. Meet Lucy!"

A loud cheer swept through the crowd and I felt myself blushing bright red.

James placed his mouth directly next to my ear and said "Welcome to the family." and with that, Lucien turned the amp back up to full volume and James continued singing into the pitch black microphone in his right hand, shooting a look at me every once in a while.


This. Was. *Heaven.*


*Around an hour later.*

After the last lyric, beat and note of 'Your Last Goodbye's performance had come to an end, there was an almost deafening cheer from the surrounding Vampires.

James replaced the microphone on its stand in the front centre of the stage and trotted down to meet us.

"So, how was-" He started, directing his question at me, but before he could finish, I launched myself at him, wrapping my arms around his neck.

"It was AMAZING! Thank you!"

He chuckled, hugging me back.

I released him, blushing slightly at my sudden outburst. I had simply been so thankful for how he acted because my dream was merely to see him again, and what he had done surpassed any dream I could ever had created in my mind and shot straight through to a life changing event.

"You're more than welcome Lucy. In fact it was my pleasure. I knew you were special from the first time I met you. Obviously I knew that you were Helena's sister, but that wasn't the reason I spoke to you that night: You have a spark." He smiled, pulling me into a one armed hug and said "Well, I'm just happy to have met you Lucy. I could tell a lot about you from the letter you wrote."

I could feel myself once again beaming as I was the happiest I had ever been in my life; the man that had been a lifeline for me for the past three years currently had his arm around me; my sister that I had previously believed to be dead, was stood on my other side; I was dressed in the best quality leather clothing, blending in with those around me, finally fitting in somewhere in my life.

My life felt complete, like nothing could go wrong.

Except it did.

Suddenly, the walls holding back the terrified emotions of my impending death crumbled, and the darkness once again flooded my mind. I fell to the floor, an agonising pain firing up and down my spine in quick succession, not stopping for a second. The world slowed and I felt a small flow of blood escape my nose as my vision faded. Helena's terrified expression was the last thing I saw.

Pain.

That was the first thing I registered as I regained consciousness.

It took me a moment to realise that the pain was coming from the right side of my neck. My eyes were closed, and my body was completely paralysed.

Accepting the fact that something had me in restraints, I attempted to pinpoint what exactly was causing the pain and in that moment, it had disappeared.

Fear slowly crept into my mind as I realised that I was in a house full of Vampires, and I was possibly the only human in the building...

Fear turned to sheer terror when my mind finally latched onto the fact that the pain, which had previously been emanating strongly from my neck, had been a *bite*.

Suddenly my lack of movement became not a mild annoyance, but a trait that was perhaps endangering my life.

There was a Vampire *right* next to me... One that had my blood in its throat and could kill me in the blink of an eye...

Terrifying thoughts swarmed my mind as I feared for my life, until a familiar voice entered my earshot.

"Irina? Is Lucy awake- IRINA?! What the *hell* are you doing?!" James's voice changed from one of concerned curiosity to downright fire.

I heard the tap of high heels on the floor.

"James." Came a silky, slightly Russian accented, feminine voice. "Darling, she is *human*."

"You didn't answer my question." He was no longer shouting, but even from where I was laid I could sense a deep, burning anger emanating from him.

She sighed deeply. "James." She started again. "Humans are food. Is that not why you invited her into this house?"

"Like *hell* it is! She is a guest, Irina! *Not* your personal blood bag!"

"Well dear. That's all humans are: Food."

"GET OUT!" His temper finally took a hold of him.

She sighed deeply again. "If you wish, darling." I heard the painfully slow *click click click* of her heels as she exited the room.

I then sensed James appear at my side and I felt him dabbing at my neck with a tissue, muttering.

"Oh god Lucy. I am so sorry."

I felt a tiny shock come from his hand the second he touched my skin, and it was obvious that he had felt it too, because he stopped dead in his tracks for a moment.

Without touching me again, I heard him cross the room, followed by the metallic thud of a bin lid closing as he disposed of the bloody tissue.

When he returned, I was able to twitch my fingers and he noticed this, breathing a sigh of relief. "You're awake."

My eyelids felt as though they were sealed shut and it was almost impossible for me to open them, but a few moments later, I had managed it. My vision was extremely blurry and at first everything was unclear, but as time passed, my eyes became adjusted and I could clearly make out the cream painted ceiling and the chandelier positioned in the centre of it.

James's face suddenly entered my vision.

I blinked slowly and moved my eyes to meet his.

"Guys." James turned away from me and looked towards the doorway "She's awake."

"Lucy!" Helena shrieked, running over to me.

I could now turn my head, and I noticed that Lucien had also entered the room with her.

"Lucy, are you alright?!" She commanded, looking over my body. Her voice suddenly became icy. "Why is there a bite mark on your neck?"

"Irina." James spat, speaking the word as though it was poison.

"She bit my *sister?!*" Helena yelled, turning to face James. "Where the hell is she?!"

"Helena, calm down." Lucien muttered, emerging further into the room.

"How can I be calm?! She BIT LUCY!"

"I know, but there is nothing we can do about it. Just calm down. We will sort this with my father later."

"'We'll sort it later'?! What is that supposed to mean!? She fed without permission on Lucy!" She gestured towards me, shouting aggressively.

Lucien grabbed her by the arm and lead her from the room, muttering "Lucy does *not* need this, especially because –"

I couldn't hear what Lucien said after that as he had disappeared from my earshot, but the start of what he was saying was enough to arouse a sense of suspicion and curiosity within me.

"James." I started, my voice only just above a whisper. "What's going on?"

He didn't say anything as he walked over to the long wooden table that I was laid on, pulling up a chair to sit beside me. He stared at his clenched hands for a moment, before looking up at me. "You nearly died." He stated, his eyebrows furrowed lightly. His piercing blue eyes were bright with concern as they locked onto mine, and he asked "What was Helena's human form dying of?"

"Cancer." I responded quietly.

"Interesting." He responded, leaning back against the hard wood of his tall backed chair.

"How is it interesting?" I asked, confused by the way the conversation had turned.

"It's interesting because Vampire blood doesn't cure cancer. It merely speeds it up, causing the patient more harm. Their inevitable death occurring prematurely."

I frowned and I lifted my head slowly from the wood. I moved my arms back and managed to force my body up from my elbows. James leaned forward and stood up, helping me into a sitting position.

"That doesn't make sense." I started, shifting uncomfortably on the table, my entire back feeling as though it had been pounded repeatedly by a large hammer. "She had begun coughing up blood. Those weren't the symptoms of her cancer. If Vampire blood speeds up the process, then–"

"Yeah." He cut me off. "It wasn't cancer. Helena was dying of something else, something that even Isaac couldn't identify."

"So what was it?" I asked, my eyebrows drawn together in confusion.

"I have no idea." He responded, a similar expression on his own face.

I sat and stared down at my hands for a moment, thinking, when another thought entered my mind.

"James. What was the shock that we both felt earlier?"

"I don't know." He replied quickly, not meeting my gaze.

"I don't believe you." I responded.

"I...have a suspicion, but it can't be true."

Suddenly he froze, his eyes wide. His head snapped up and he came within centimetres of my face, looking desperately in my eyes, searching for something.

"Oh crap. Lucy-"

Before he could say any more, I fell off the table and onto the ground, a sharp pain shooting up my legs. But I could not process it as my entire body had been invaded by another agonizing, torturous pain, unlike anything I had experienced before.

I felt a burning, tearing sensation in the left side of my chest and it felt as though something was working its way up my body.

I couldn't breathe.

Something was blocking my airway. It was certain now that a large object was forcing its way through my system and whatever it was, felt barbed. I could almost feel the inside of my body being cut open wherever the unknown substance passed.

I felt like I was dying and I clawed at my throat, feeling it almost in my mouth. I knew that within moments the vile, torturous object would be out, and I closed my eyes, attempting to endure the pain. I failed, unable to scream or take a single breath due to the obstruction.

Just as I thought I would faint from the pain, I felt a roughly circular shaped, smooth, soft, fleshy substance fall against the back of my teeth. I immediately spat it out onto the floor and I had only a couple of seconds to gaze at it in confusion, shock, and horror before I felt another surge of pain from my chest. It seemed as though another one of those *things* was detaching itself from my heart.

This time, the disgusting globule found its exit in half the time and I fell to the floor, exhausted.

James reached down to me and the second he touched me, a shock shot across my skin like lightning, much stronger than before. He immediately withdrew his hand.

"This isn't possible." He muttered, eyes wide and shaking his head in denial. "No."

"James." I breathed, still recovering. "What. Is. Happening?!"

Ignoring the intense shock that erupted across both of our bodies, James grabbed me and hauled me into a standing position. He slowly brought his hand up to my neck. As the seconds ticked by, I saw his eyes take on a hard, stony exterior. Around thirty seconds later, he lowered his hand, shaking slightly.

"Lucy. I am so sorry."

"What is wrong with me?" I muttered, terrified by the entire situation. My voice also seemed muffled, but I ignored it.

James took my arm and led me to a mirror that hung upon the wall at the opposite side of the room.

As we neared the reflective surface I stared in confusion at my appearance.

Because the thing I saw reflected there was not my face.

My *reflection* was a monster...

My *reflection* had pitch black eyes...

My *reflection* had deathly pale skin...

The worst part was that my reflection had long, curved, canine teeth that stretched to just below its bottom lip.

No, my reflection wasn't a monster...

It was a Vampire.

# CHAPTER SIX

"No..." I breathed, bringing my hands up to my face and feeling around my fangs. "This is not possible." A sense of awe, fear and confusion entered my mind as I gazed into the deep black pits of my eyes.

James slowly walked away from me, not having said anything. He progressed to sit down gently in a tall backed, wooden chair.

"But it is." He replied eventually, his voice monotone.

James rested his elbow on the oak table and then placed his chin on his slender fingers. His eyes appeared to be unfocussed and glazed over, as if thinking deeply.

"You're a Vampire." He muttered, still lost in his own train of thought.

I shuffled slowly over to him, and the longer I looked at his face, the quicker I realised that he wasn't only lost in thought: He was attempting to conceal an emotion of horrified confusion.

"James?" I asked, crouching down to try and put myself in his line of vision.

Within a second, his electric blue eyes flashed to meet mine, and in that instant he shot up from his seat and grabbed me by the shoulders.

He hoisted me up to a standing position, an extreme shock flashing across both of our skins.

"Do you feel that?!" James demanded, his eyes having taken on a desperate look.

"Yes, but–"

He cut me off. "That is *wrong!*"

"What do you mean?!" I asked him, my voice having gained a tone of distress. "How is this wrong?!"

He roughly released me and paced across the wooden floorboards, running his hand through his hair.

"What's wrong is that you're *mine*, Lucy! You are my Vampire! I turned you!"

I withdrew into myself slightly at his shouts, but I was able to ask him "how is that possible?"

"That's the problem, I don't know." He took a deep breath and threw himself back down into his chair. "I have no bloody idea. The worst part of all this, is that because it was my blood that transformed you, you are mine in more than one way. We share the Lythia bond, Lucy." On his last word he looked directly at me, a pained, tired, scared look in his eyes.

"Which means...She's going to kill you. My mother... She's already on her way."

I opened my mouth to say something, but I was unable to utter a single word, my mind having become a complete blank at his news. Instead, I just brought my eyebrows together in confusion and let him continue explaining the situation.

James now looked down at his slightly shaking, clasped hands. "She will do it... Trust me, I have witnessed it first hand: She killed the woman that Lucien had transformed into a Vampire and fallen in love with. She murdered the woman who was pregnant with his child."

My eyes widened "What?"

James nodded slightly "She slaughtered Lucien's love and her own unborn grandson in the blink of an eye. She has no limits and forcing pain and distress upon others brings her happiness. She's an unstoppable monster who desires power above anything and everything else."

"...and she's coming to kill me." I clarified, seating myself at the table, pushing my head into my hands. "What the hell did I do?" I asked, shaking my head.

I had never done anything to anyone to ever warrant them a desire to kill me. Since both my father's and Helena's passing, I had always been the broken, sad, lonely girl that no-one talked to, let alone hated enough to want dead.

I didn't understand.

Yet there was just *so* much that I didn't understand in this twisted world. In comparison to the ancient creatures who resided in the area around me, I was naive. Before I had transformed, to them I was food.

That was the most confusing thing of all: They are just like humans, only with fangs, heightened senses and immortality. Every single other thing was the same. We think the same. We walk the same grounds and we are touched by the same magic of the natural, unexplainable beauty of this planet that we will never truly be able to understand. We have the same emotions: Fear, love, hatred, jealousy, anger, despair... Yet they still think that they can rip the life from the surrounding 'walking blood bags' that are humans.

"No." I stated, my voice stronger than I had anticipated.

I pulled my head up from out of my hands and looked hard at James until his weary eyes met my own.

"No." I repeated. "She's not going to kill me. She may have the power and the strength. But I have the one thing that she will never have: A reason for surviving." My soul began burning with anger "I have been through more than she could ever imagine." My breathing became slightly ragged, but it only fuelled my rage-filled speech "I am stronger than she will ever know. She will *not* rip this life from me. I lost my human life to unknown reasons, but I sure as hell am not giving this one up. I am a Vampire. That makes me strong. That makes me powerful, and that makes me dangerous." My voice had risen to a shout as I yelled further at James. "Your mother may have murdered hundreds, perhaps thousands of people, but she has never come across me. Even in my human form, when rage, pure rage, filled me, I knew that I had the capacity to kill someone with my own bare hands. If someone had touched anyone I cared about, I would have ripped them to pieces. Now I am a Vampire." I shook my head, resorting back to my natural Vampire form "AND I LOOK LIKE THIS! I have these fangs. I have this strength." I grabbed the chair that I had been sat on, and with a flick of my wrist, I tore one of the legs off, proceeding to throw the rest of it against the wall, turning it to splinters. "I can heal any wound." I stabbed the chair leg through the palm of my left hand, before tearing it back out of my skin and launching the thin piece of wood across the room to where the rest of its body had fallen, all the while keeping eye contact with James. "I am immortal, James. I don't age. I don't get sick. I don't get hurt." I slammed both of my hands down on the wooden table "I failed to protect those that I loved before due to weakness. I will *never* be weak again. No-one I love will ever die due to my lack of power." I took a deep, shaky breath, still staring at him.

"I have never met her." I started, my voice lowering back down to the volume of normal speech. "But she killed your nephew and Lucien's partner." I stood back up straight. "She cannot be forgiven for that. From what else you have said about her, she *is* a monster."

James nodded, his black hair falling slightly over the right side of his face. "She is." He muttered, gazing at me with a look that reflected sympathy, awe, confusion and also pride.

"Then it's time the tables turned. Lucien lost everything because of her. It's time we return the favour." I felt a fiery, determined rage once again enter my system. "We are going to destroy the one thing she cannot live without: Her power. She broke Lucien's heart, so I'll break hers. Just in a more literal sense: I will rip her cold, black, poisoned heart from her chest and I will watch the light leave her eyes, watch the despair enter her soul when she realises that a mere, unimportant Vampire has ended her pathetic excuse of a life, halting her power-fuelled existence." I took a deep breath. "Then I'll crush it, and you and Lucien will finally be free."

Even in my Vampire form, my outburst of pure, uncontrolled rage had left me exhausted and I leant on the table to keep myself upright.

I placed both hands on the wood and closed my eyes, breathing deeply.

Unable to stand upright, I slowly lowered myself to the ground, leaning the back of my head against the table, having blanked out the entire world.

*Breathe, Lucy.* I thought to myself. *You've done this before. Just not with the same amount of power.*

Drawing my knees up to my chest, I continued breathing deeply.

"Lucy." Came a voice from behind me.

There it was. That was what brought me back:

His voice.

As if my body had been drained of all distress and anger, I rose from the ground and faced him.

James had stood up and walked over to me, his pale eyes looking hard into mine.

"Lucy." He repeated, walking closer to me and putting his hand on the side of my arm.

An electrifying shock shot between the two of us, but unlike before it felt comforting, like I belonged.

Without saying anything, he wrapped his arms protectively around me.

I took a deep breath, leaning my head against his shoulder.

"I'm sorry." I muttered into his jacket.

He pulled back from me and looked up and down the features of my face, brushing away a strand of hair and keeping his right hand on my cheek. "Don't be."

"Lucy Brown." He sighed, lowering his hand to place it back around my waist. "You are one of the strongest people I have ever met. I told you this on the first day we saw each other: You deserve the strength that you have built up. That still applies to this day. You were an outcast, someone that people ignored and tormented, someone torn apart by despair and sadness. You could have gone off the deep end. You could have lost it all. But instead you painstakingly, piece by shattered piece, put yourself back together. You are not the same girl as you were three years ago. I will never be able to understand how you pulled yourself back from the edge, but all I can do is congratulate and envy you."

"Do you really not know what kept me from going under?" I asked him, astonishment on my face.

He shook his head.

"You." I said simply. "Your voice. The music that you, Chris, Damian, Josh and Ben made. You, and the other members of 'Your Last Goodbye' kept me alive."

"How?" He asked, his eyebrows furrowing.

We had both dropped our arms by now and were stood apart from each other.

"You arrived at a time I needed you the most." I smiled, reminiscing on the time when I was just a simple human with admiration for a band. "Although you never knew that I existed, and I was only one of thousands of people whose life you had touched, it didn't matter. Even though, at the time, I thought we would never meet and that I would never mean anything to you, your music made me feel like I wasn't alone. That is more than anyone has ever done for me. So thank you, James."

A small frown remained on his face, but he once again hugged me to his chest.

"I don't understand how we do what you say, but I am glad that we help."

I pulled back "It's because your emotions are so raw when you're singing. The writing of the lyrics involves all five of you. I don't know. I can just *feel* you all within your music. I always have been able to read people, and I have always been able to understand them even when they don't speak their minds. To me, the songs that your band produces are literally your pure emotions leaking out of the music. When I was upset, your words made me feel as though I wasn't completely alone in my life, and also, your uplifting lyrics brought me back to thinking positively when I had felt that the entire world was turning against me. I can't place it. I've never been able to. When I try and explain to people how you saved me, I have no words."

"You really are something, Lucy." He smiled at me before adding "Well. You say that all five of us saved you?"

I nodded.

"I think it's time that you met the rest of them."

He led me into the main room where I had previously spent the night singing, dancing and laughing with my sister and a group of strangers. The last time I was in that room, I had still been *normal*.

Now, I was anything other than normal, but I didn't care.

My Vampirism, this strength, was a beautiful blessing – I could never see it as a curse.

We made our way over to a table in the corner of the room, around which sat four men, all wearing leather, their black hair styled in a variety of ways.

"Hey guys. Meet Lucy!"

They all turned and chorused a greeting.

Chris got up and bounded towards me, quickly wrapping his arms around my waist and picking me up. "Hey girl!"

"Uh, hi Chris!" I replied, shocked by his sudden action, a giggle escaping my throat. I returned the hug, patting him on the back. He pulled back from me, his shaggy black hair falling across his heavily defined cheekbones. "You know my name? I'm flattered!"

I nodded. "Of course I do. I know all of you." I looked at each face of the band members in front of me, before adding "and I mean that in a completely non-creepy stalker way." Chris chuckled. "I like her, James! This chick's got a sense of humour on her!"

"Sounds good." Ben piped up. "But the question is, can she hold her liquor?"

"Ah." Josh laughed. "The induction."

I frowned, and Damian enlightened me "We kind of have this thing where if we meet someone, we have to test their tolerance to alcohol."

My frown deepened. "Okay?"

"We're a rock and roll band, girl." James gave me a mischievous half smile.

"You're not dropping out are you?" Ben asked.

"Oh, not at all. I've done shots before. Granted, I was by myself, but still."

A joint groan came from the group of men. "You drank alone? Not cool, dude." Chris exclaimed.

"Agreed. We're getting you hammered." Ben nodded, shooting up from his seat. He grabbed me by the arm and led me to a long, mahogany bar, behind which stood a tall, masculine man, adorning a tight fitting, black, button up shirt.

The bartender shot me a wide grin and placed down the pint glass that he was drying before throwing the towel over his left shoulder.

"So what'll it be?" He asked.

As Ben was about to place an order, I quickly interjected.

"Vodka. Lots and lots of vodka."

"I would ask for ID but I think we're past that here."

Ben gave me an approving look before turning to James.

"I hope you're not wanting to make a move on this girl: I think I'm gonna marry her."

James chuckled, moving to stand in between Ben and myself.

"Don't worry, Luc, I'll keep you from Benjamin's clutches." He winked at me before addressing the long line of shot glasses filled with a clear liquid.

"Alright, everyone get one."

Still grinning, I grabbed the closest glass to me and held it in my hand, waiting for the others to take their own. Once everyone had taken their own glass, Ben looked around to make sure.

"Everyone ready? Alright. You first new girl."

In one swift motion I flicked my head back, tipping the small glass quickly. I quickly swallowed the fiery substance before smashing the glass back down on the wood.

Except I actually smashed it.

"James?" Ben turned to look at him expectantly.

"Yeah." He replied, awkwardly. "There's something I haven't told you guys."

"I gathered." Ben shot him a scolding look.

"Hey." I interrupted. "I am right here. But it's fine, honestly Ben. I love being one of you already. Don't ruin tonight, please."

As Ben was thinking of objecting, Chris pushed forward and downed his shot like a hungry wolf.

"Woohoo! Who's next?"

I gave Chris a thanking look before everyone else followed suit.

James was the last to take his, but as he raised the glass to his mouth, he made eye contact with me, checking to see if I was alright.

Nodding to indicate that I was perfectly happy, I turned back to the growing line of alcohol.

"At least I have a higher tolerance now. Let's do this."

Although I was physically strong, Ben still drank me under the table.

"Okay, I'm done!" I shouted, throwing up my arms, giggling and overbalancing slightly.

"Pretty good for a first time with us." Ben slurred.

"Yep!" Chris agreed, sitting up quickly from the floor, cradling an empty pint glass in his hand, which he had acquired half way through the evening. Almost immediately he slumped back down to the floor, hugging the glass like a soft toy, and within moments we heard loud snoring.

I began giggling uncontrollably while indicating to Chris.

"What is it?" James asked.

"He–!" I struggled to form a coherent sentence due to my fit of laughter and obvious intoxication, so I simply pointed to Chris's sleeping form.

James raised one eyebrow, obviously entertained by my drunken state.

"Let's get you to sleep."

"But! I'm a Vampire now! No sleep for me! Who wants tequila?!" I shouted, my words merging together, raising my hand to get the bartender's attention.

"I think she's had enough." James explained as he arrived, placing his arm around my waist and half dragging me towards the door.

"What? Where are we going? The bar's that way." I frowned at him, confused.

"Yeah, I know. We're getting you to bed now."

"Ugh, boring." I muttered, leaning into him, my eyes drooping.

"See? You're tired."

"No I'm not." I denied, almost unconscious.

James just shook his head and chuckled as he more or less carried me from the room.


(James)

I sighed as I picked up her unconscious form.

I had known that Ben's famous 'induction' would have completely taken it out of her, even as a Vampire.

As I reached the bottom of the staircase, I halted for a moment before deciding to deliver her to Helena. It was probably the best place for her to rest and get mocked for being completely hammered.

A few minutes later I arrived at Helena's door. Not bothering to knock, I turned the handle and pushed against the wood.

"Hope you don't mind, Helena, she drank – Whoa!"

I had just walked in on Lucien and Helena in bed together.

"James!" She shrieked, pulling the covers tight around her naked figure.

"Sorry!" I exclaimed, turning my head to the side, away from them.

"You tool, get out James." Came Lucien's gruff voice.

"Fine by me." I replied quickly, turning out into the corridor and closing the door behind me.

I shook my head profusely, trying to clear the previous image from my mind.

"That was weird." I muttered to myself.

I decided that I would let her rest in my own room as she would be awake within the hour due to her improved metabolism.

I switched the lights on as I entered, and a bright glow filled the room, causing me to wince.

Apparently the alcohol had affected me more than I had realised.

Placing Lucy gently down on my crimson sheets, I looked over her unconscious figure, tilting my head slightly.

I frowned, remembering her aggressive outburst.

I recalled how she told me that she had experienced a lot of emotional pain due to the death of her father and Helena's disappearance. But her strength still amazed and, in a way, unnerved me. It made me feel that way because she reminded me of my mother. Lucy didn't want to be weak and my mother desired power.

I shook my head, standing next to her.

No, she wasn't like my mother at all. I looked over her dark hair, her almost childlike features, and her heavy lashes. Her eyes were what captivated my attention the most: They had cried a thousand tears, been witness to her abuse at school, but they still regained their unique light. She was a fresh, powerful young woman who, I believed, was what we needed to take my mother down. My eyes slowly began to droop, the alcohol having caught up with me.

"Yeah, I'm going to get some sleep." I muttered to myself, walking around the other side of my bed and laying down gently on my side, facing Lucy.

I vowed to keep one ear open as I slept, to protect her in case my mother arrived.

Although I didn't doubt Lucy's strength, I knew that my mother was *extremely* powerful and if Lucy was to in fact kill her, she would need my help. I would protect this girl to my death, not just because she was the only person that I could transform into *my* Vampire, which automatically connected us with the Lythia bond, but because she deserved my protection: She had protected herself for years against the many horrors of this world, and now it was our turn to help her. She claimed that we made her feel as though she wasn't alone. Well, now she certainly wasn't: She was part of our family.


(Lucy)

I inhaled deeply through my nose, rolling over onto my left side.

"What a nice dream." I muttered to myself, my eyes still closed.

Wondering what time it was, and if I was missing school, I rolled back onto my right side and opened my eyes. My hand found air where my bedside table should have been.

I frowned and looked around.

It turned out that I wasn't in my own room, in fact I was in a large, brightly lit one with a chandelier hanging from the centre of the ceiling. On the walls hung framed record albums.

I had no idea where I was, and as I was about to get up, I saw, out the corner of my eye, the figure of someone laid beside me.

I froze, not moving an inch.

Who the hell was beside me? Where was I?

Slowly, my eyes wide, I turned my head to the left, and who I saw there made my mouth hang open.

James Killoran.

I was in bed with James Killoran.

My eyes still wide, I shuffled further up the bed so that I was leant against the wooden headboard.

I eyed his sleeping figure with suspicion.

What had happened and more importantly, *why* was I sharing a bed with him?

We didn't...?

I suddenly realised that I had no memory of the previous night or how I got there. All I remembered was taking a few shots with Ben – Crap. I had gotten completely smashed.

I let out a loud sigh and banged my head against the headboard behind me.

"Good one." I muttered to myself.

So I had met five of the most important men in my life, and I got drunk and probably passed out.

"I'm such a lightweight."

"Not exactly." James muttered, his eyes still closed.

"Really?" I questioned him, drawing my eyebrows together, concerned that I had seemed pathetic to them all.

He opened his eyes, his pale blue irises immediately taking my breath away again.

"Really. You beat Chris and Josh. Damian decided to grab some scotch and went to watch the sun rise. He likes to think he's wise."

I chuckled. "I'm pretty impressed that I beat Chris to be fair. From what I seen, he seemed like quite the party animal."

"Nah." James let out a deep breath, closing his eyes again "He's more of an excited puppy."

"You still hung over?" I asked.

"Mmhm." He confirmed, nodding slightly.

"Sounds like I beat you too, then."

He opened one eye to look at me.

"I get a pass – I carried you up here." He informed me, before closing his eye again.

"Ah, okay. Thanks." I frowned. At least I had an answer to my question of 'how did I get here?'

I thought for a moment, and decided to bite the bullet and ask him the question that had been playing on my mind. "So I'm guessing I passed out... We didn't... do anything, did we?" I queried.

He now opened both eyes to look at me, his face straight.

"I don't know what you mean."

"I mean, like... *anything.*"

"I still don't follow."

I pulled an uncomfortable face, and I felt myself blushing, attempting to give him an informative answer.

Suddenly a warm smile crossed his face. "Calm down, I know what you mean, and no, we didn't."

"Okay. Glad we got that cleared up." I nodded, still flustered.

"I don't go for girls while they're in a comatose state." He muttered.

Wait. Did that mean he would have if I was awake–

Why the hell was I thinking about that, what was wrong with me? I loved this man just for *existing* and making me happy. I was not about to start thinking like *that* about him, no matter how attractive he was.

"I need some air." I muttered, standing from the bed and walking over to a set of ceiling to floor length, heavy, crimson curtains. Without thinking, I pulled them back to reveal a bright ray of sunlight.

"CRAP!" I yelled, running from the bright light, suddenly remembering that I was a Vampire.

I heard a soft chuckle come from the bed.

"It's not funny!" I shrieked.

"It really is." James responded, rolling over and sitting up on the side of the bed.

I shot him an extremely unimpressed look, while pressing myself into the wall, in an attempt to keep away from the sunlight as much as possible.

"It is, look." He slowly walked across the room, and I realised that he was about to walk directly into the sun's rays.

"What are you doing?!" I exclaimed, indicating to the bright lines of sunlight on the wooden floor.

He continued walking, without paying any attention.

He was almost into dangerous territory, so I ran across the floor and shoved into him, pushing him out of the way. I had misjudged my weight distribution and ended up shoving us both to the ground.

I rolled off him immediately.

"What were you doing?! It's *sunlight!*" I scolded him.

"and you ran through it to protect me?" He queried, looking at me in confusion.

"Of course I did!" I exclaimed, not seeing why he was acting so strange.

"You knew that the sun's rays were dangerous, yet you passed through them to keep me from getting harmed?"

"Yes, and I'd do it again." I replied, impatient.

A small smile crossed his lips. "You truly are completely selfless."

I suddenly realised what he was talking about, and my concern fell from my mind.

I shook my head. "No, I'm completely the opposite. I am extremely selfish: I've lost too many people I love and care about. Now that I'm a Vampire, I have more of a chance of keeping them safe. I'm selfish because I can't lose anyone else."

"So you 'love and care' about me, huh?" He queried, lifting the mood.

I jokingly shoved into him. "Trust you to focus on that."

My face suddenly fell and I lifted a hand to my stomach.

I was *hungry*.

"Ah." He began, realising what was happening. "Yeah, you're a Vampire now... Your breakfast isn't pancakes anymore..."

"Yeah, I hadn't really thought about that."

"Well, you've a Vampire Lucy. It kind of comes with the package. I'd offer you a blood bag, but since you're new to this, I think it's worth taking you out on a hunt."

I frowned, indicating to the bright rays of sunlight, streaming through the window to our side. "How?"

"Oh yeah. We're immune."

"What?!"

"Because I turned you, you are a 'born-Vampire' like me. As the name suggests, we were *born* as Vampires, so we have special skills."

"Hang on." I held up a hand as all of my facts about Vampires fell to dust in my mind. "So you can walk in sunlight? You were *born*, not turned? Now I remember it, you can have children too?"

He nodded. "Only born Vampires can though. Don't worry, the last three years of your life researching hasn't been a waste – normal Vampires follow almost every rule in the lore books. Naturally, they can't walk in the sunlight, but we have a few sorcerers living five minutes away who can make daylight pendants."

"So the whole point of stressing me out, thinking that I was going to die in sunlight, was just funny to you?"

"Yeah, it kinda' was."

"I hate you." I replied, once again blessing him with my unimpressed facial expression.

"No you don't. Right. Food."

"Yeah... food." I clarified, a look of distaste on my face.

"Oh don't worry about it. I will make this as painless as possible. Elaine's coming too – She heard you were going out and she wants to take you shopping."

"Sounds about right." I agreed, remembering Elaine's obvious obsession with material objects.

*Knock knock.*

We both turned our heads in the direction of the door, around which Helena appeared.

"Hey guys."

"Well hello Helena, nice to see you clothed for a change." James raised his eyebrows at her.

I frowned at him and shot her a confused look.

She immediately flushed a deep red.

"Yeah, Lucy. I'm kind of with Lucien... and James saw me *with* Lucien last night."

"No." I held up a hand, shaking my head roughly. "Don't want to know anymore."

"That's probably for the better." She replied awkwardly.

"So Helena!" I exclaimed, quickly trying to change the subject "James is taking me out for breakfast, and Elaine's taking me shopping. Do you want to come?"

"Yeah, why not!" She replied, probably more excitably than necessary. I could see the thanks in her eyes at me for changing the conversation topic.

"Girls are weird." James muttered. "I'll just stand there and feel like I want to die the entire time, okay?"

"Sounds like a plan." I nodded.

# CHAPTER SEVEN

O h this is so exciting Lucy!" Elaine clapped as I lowered myself into the passenger seat.

"There really are some *amazing* shops here!" She continued, an elated look on her face.

While his hands rested on the steering wheel, James raised one eyebrow in my direction.

I shot him a look that said 'shut-up', as I was letting Elaine have her day of dressing both Helena and myself up in pretty clothes.

My sister quickly jumped in the car "Hey guys! Sorry about that! Lucien saw me-"

"Don't want to know!" I repeated, interrupting her and she once again blushed, beaming.

"This is going to be wonderful girls!" Elaine piped up, a wide grin on her face.

"Yeah, for you, I'm sure it will be." James muttered, turning the keys and pulling out of the drive.

"James!" She scolded. "This is Lucy's first shopping trip! Do I need to send you to the salon again? How about a manicure?"

"Okay, I'll stop." He replied quickly.

Was that *fear* I saw on his face?

I simply shook my head, smiling as I turned to look out of the window.

Twenty minutes later, we pulled into a massive, busy car park.

"Okay. First of all we're sorting Lucy's breakfast." James began.

A look of distaste crossed my face "Yeah. Great." I muttered.

"Hey, you said you were fine with being one of us–"

"Wait, what?! What do you mean 'one of us'?!" Helena demanded.

I suddenly recalled that I hadn't told either of them about my transformation.

I fell silent and James gave me a look of awkward concern. "I think we're all going to need a drink to stomach this information."

"Yes." I replied shortly, quickly getting out of the car and walking across the tarmac.

Crap. Crap. Crap. I had completely forgotten to tell them. I felt so *stupid..* How were they going to take it?! Helena would go crazy at me for keeping it from her!

My eyes scanned the surrounding shops and they fell upon a small pub. That was the building in which I would tell them. It was also probably where I was going to have my first 'meal' as a Vampire.

I groaned inwardly at the thought of drinking a human's blood. What would it taste like? Would I like it? Would it make me feel sick, due to the fact that I had been a human myself, mere hours ago? Would my powers be enhanced or would I be the same? Would anything special happen?

"Lucy, breathe." James grabbed my arm.

Jumping at his touch, I spun around to face him.

"What do you mean?! Hunting a human? Yeah, I'm completely fine. This isn't weird at all!" I gasped, having been shocked at his quick appearance.

He just looked at me.

"What!"

110

"You just Vamp ran. You're stressing."

I looked over his shoulder to see Helena and Elaine only a couple of strides away from the car, which was now around forty metres away from me.

"Well maybe I am James. Less than 24 hours ago, I was human. Now I'm about to go and feed one on one of them. Are you not aware of how uncomfortable that makes me?"

"Yeah, but you'll learn. It's alright. You're just higher up the food chain now. That's all."

"Yeah. I know." I replied shortly. "and it freaks me out."

"It shouldn't. I'll make sure that you don't really hurt anyone and it will all be okay, trust me."

"That isn't what I'm worried about! I have researched everything about Vampires for the past three years, so I know how they feed. Granted, the actual fangs are slightly bigger, but that doesn't change anything. No, what makes me feel uncomfortable is that *because* I researched them for such a long time, I always saw them as another *species*: Something *completely* different to a human. Now? I'm one of them. Do you not understand? I became a fictional character from within a book."

"You talk about Vampires a lot as 'they', but Lucy you're right, you *are* one now, so refer to 'them' as 'us' because you can't change that fact." He replied bluntly, but in a kind voice.

I sighed. "I know, and I wouldn't, even if I had the choice – You know I love this power, but let me have a day to get used to it."

Helena and Elaine caught up to us.

"I think you have some explaining to do Lucy!" My sister commanded, expectantly.

I nodded. "You will get your explanation – as much as I know, anyway – but not here." I turned around and pointed to the pub I had originally had my eye on. "I'll tell you in there. Let's go."

I walked to the back corner of the building and found a quiet booth, sectioned apart from the rest of the area by two walls. Sitting in the far back corner, I cleared the sauce sachets and menus away to the side, attempting to pass the time until the others arrived, my mind on other things.

How on earth was I going to tell my sister that I was a *Vampire*?! Would they try and find a way to make me human again? Would they try and make me regret the happiness I had experienced due to my transformation?

I had no idea.

Seconds later, James came into view and sat beside me, closely followed by Helena and Elaine, who sat on the opposite side of the table. Without saying anything, Helena sat opposite me, shooting me a hard look.

"Right..." James started, trying to make the solid silence less painful. "So Lucy's a Vampire."

"How the hell did this happen?!" Helena demanded, breaking her momentary silence.

"I have no idea." I replied quietly.

"Who turned you?"

I took a deep breath, preparing myself. I looked at James briefly before sheepishly turning to Helena.

"James...apparently."

Helena turned slowly to face him, a deadly expression on her face "Why?! What is *wrong* with you? She was happy as a human!"

"Actually-"

"SHUT UP!" She interrupted me. "James. You killed my sister. I had an excuse – Isaac tried to cure my cancer and it went wrong. That's why *I* am a Vampire. What was your reason for turning Lucy?!"

James shrugged and shook his head "I honestly don't remember doing it."

"You *forgot*?!" She almost screamed at him.

"No, I mean it was like it never happened. I have absolutely *no* recollection of even contemplating turning her."

"Well that makes no bloody sense! How can you just *forget* something like that?! If you haven't already gathered, you are a born–Vampire. That means that Lucy is too. You share the Lythia bond, meaning that the two of you are joined forever. Why would you turn Lucy if you knew that would happen?!"

"I don't know!" James replied, the distress at the gap in his memory that he had been attempting so desperately to conceal, pushed through to the surface.

"There could be an explanation." Elaine said slowly, locking eyes with James. "and I think you already know what it is."

He shook his head. "No. She hasn't been here in over a century."

"Not that you know of." She replied shortly.

"Wait, who are you talking about?" I queried.

"Victoria." Elaine responded, almost spitting the word out.

"Who is...?"

"My mother." James informed me, not moving his eyes from Elaine. "I told you that she was powerful Lucy. She can control even *our* minds." He then turned to me. "That's what Elaine is referring to: She believes that my mother could have taken my memory of turning you."

He once again turned his gaze back to Elaine.

"But that's not possible. She was a *human* when she came here, *not* a Dhampir."

"That's what it *looked* like, you are correct. But your mother has been meddling in powerful witchcraft for the past two decades. She could have placed a cloaking enchantment upon her, to conceal her Vampirism. Was there a point in which something strange happened since you arrived at this house?" Elaine looked questioningly at me.

I was about to say 'no', when my mind flashed back to the torturous pain that had emanated from my chest, only to then end with me producing two spherical globules. My face fell as I remembered that *that* was the moment I had become a Vampire.

"Actually yes, There was." I began. "Last night, once I had regained consciousness, and after Irina drank my blood–" Helena made an angered snorting noise. "–I ended up throwing up these two round things."

Elaine's eyes widened slightly, her face becoming even paler than her natural Vampiric complexion.

"If that's the case, then I was correct: James could have transformed you years previously, and no-one would have known about it. You see, I studied dark witchcraft, merely as a hobby to research the 'dark side' of our powers, and I came across this enchantment that conceals someone's Vampirism within their heart. This has to be done quite quickly after the person has been transformed, as the remaining human blood in their system is stored in these... brown, fleshy spheres, each storing one litre."

I nodded. "Yeah, they felt as though they had detached themselves from my heart."

"Yes." Elaine shot a look at Helena before continuing "The point is you were never meant to know you that were a Vampire, Lucy. Victoria made sure that the orbs were strong enough to replicate your human blood, so that if you cut yourself, you wouldn't just bleed out and become a Vampire. The *only* way that the blood can be drained, faster than it can be made is if a Vampire draws it from you..."

Helena almost exploded. "IRINA WAS THE ONE WHO FORCED HER TO BE A VAMPIRE?!!"

"Yes... If it wasn't for Irina, you would still be human. When she drank your blood, the orbs no longer had anything to replicate, so they basically died."

"I'm going to kill her. I'M GOING TO BLOODY KILL HER!" Helena shouted, determinedly.

"I wouldn't bother." Elaine replied, shaking her head. "She's already dead."

"Huh?"

"Unless she drunk *exactly* two litres of Lucy's blood, she's dead. Knowing Irina, she would have consumed much more, more like three or four litres."

James suddenly began to understand. "So at least one litre of the blood she drank would have been that of a Vampire's...?"

Elaine nodded. "Exactly – Which is toxic."

"So I poisoned her?" I asked, dumbfounded.

A malicious smile spread across Helena's face.

"Yes, you did." Elaine confirmed.

"Good." Helena stated sharply. I noticed that her smile had fallen, her face having become expressionless. "She killed you and made sure that you can *never* go home to our mother. Because of this, we are going to have to fake your death: Meaning that you can never see mum again, and I personally don't think she will be able to survive losing the two of us."

I hadn't thought about that.

In my excitement of transforming into a Vampire and the power that accompanied it, I had completely forgotten about my previous, human life and all the complications that it would have on my current one.

My home seemed worlds away, my previous life appearing like a story – This, right here, was reality: Sat in a pub with three other Vampires including my twin sister, who I had two days previously believed to be dead. One of my other companions at this quiet table, out of sight from everyone, was a world-renowned rock singer of my favourite band.

It was like a twisted fantasy of a life.

The sound of Helena's phone ringing shook me from my deep thoughts. She quickly snatched it up, holding it to her ear.

She was quiet for a moment, listening to the voice on the other end and then said "Okay, we're at Dewmont Tavern." There was a brief pause "Alright, see you soon. Love you too." She muttered before hanging up.

"That was Lucien. He has some information on why you passed out last night. He had his suspicions earlier... but now he thinks he knows the actual reason." I saw her clench her teeth and I knew immediately that something was terribly wrong – That was her 'tell'.

"Well, while we wait for Lucien to arrive, I think I should get Lucy someone to eat. C'mon." He shuffled along the small sofa and stood at the end of the booth.

I was hesitant for a moment before I took a deep breath and followed him to the bar.

"Okay. The most important thing is to not look scared – You'll draw attention to yourself."

I nodded. "I'm not scared, it's just as I said before – This is weird for me."

"Well, just try and act natural."

"Okay." I muttered to myself, closing my eyes and taking a deep breath. "Natural."

At that point in time, 'natural' was a hunter, so that is what I became.

I stared hard at James. "Let me do this."

"What? Lucy it's your first time, let me choose someone-"

"No." I shook my head "You told me to be natural? I can do that. I've been researching *our* species-" I put extra emphasis on the word due to our previous conversation "-for years. I know how to be a natural Vampire."

He eyed me with concern and suspicion but nodded.

"Fine. Show me what you've got."

I smiled as I turned around, taking what he had said to be a challenge.

I pulled up a barstool next to an attractive young man who was nursing a pint of lager, and I waited for the bartender in silence.

Out of the corner of my left eye, I saw James watching me closely, but the man to my right had also taken note of me sat beside him.

He turned his head to face me, looking me up and down like I was a piece of meat.

*Ugh.* He was one of *those* guys.

"Well hello." He purred flirtatiously, flashing me a wide grin.

*Ugh.* My mind repeated in disgust.

I gave him a small smile and a quick "Hi." before looking down at my hands in my lap.

My response had the desired effect and he turned his full body towards me, leaning his right, muscular arm against the bar, bending it casually to show the full extent of his strength.

I chuckled internally at what he would call 'strength' in regard to my own.

"So are you waiting for someone?" He asked me.

I shook my head, looking back up at him and into his eyes. "No, i'm not."

"You know, you have lovely eyes."

*Ugghhh.* I groaned inwardly.

I responded with an embarrassed smile, before saying "and you... have a lovely jugular."

His own smile fell and was replaced by a confused, uncomfortable expression.

"Uh – I have to go..." He stood up to leave, but I placed a hand on his arm looked hard into his eyes.

"No. I don't think you do. I think you actually really want to stay."

"Yes." He said, almost in a trance. "I do want to stay."

"Good!" I beamed. "Now, let's get out of here." I looked at him mischievously before standing and walking towards the exit.

When I turned, I saw James gazing at me with an expression of shock, mixed with pride.

I sensed him rise from his seat as the unnamed man followed me from the building.

"Where are we going?" He asked.

"You'll see." I responded, not turning around.

Turning left sharply out of the door, I walked the length of the building before finding a small, one metre gap down the side of the pub.

I quickly stepped into it, immediately pulling him in by his white shirt. We both had our backs pressed against the bricks of the two buildings and I smiled seductively at him.

"Now. Isn't this cosy?"

His natural personality came back as he stood in front of me.

"Yeah. It is." He looked from my eyes to my lips.

He slowly leaned in and as our mouths were mere centimetres away from each others, I said "But I'm not here to kiss you... I'm here to eat you."

A confused, disgusted and uncomfortable expression crossed his face, and he was about to pull back just as I shot forward and sunk my fangs into the left side of his neck.

How could I have been concerned about *this*?!

It was the sweetest taste I had ever experienced!

I heard him making small, pained noises in response to the draining of his blood, but I ignored him, focussing on the warm, crimson liquid flowing down my throat, heightening my senses to the maximum and rejuvenating my slightly tired body.

*Stop.*

My mind suddenly commanded.

I frowned against the new voice, placing my hand on his back.

*Lucy, stop.*

I realised that it wasn't *my* mind, it was James's.

*Just a little more.*

I thought back.

*No. Stop – you don't want to kill him.*

*Don't I?*

There was a momentary silence before a painful STOP resounded around my mind. Pulling away quickly, in shock, I felt the man collapse.

I caught him under the arms and he fell against me.

I noticed the blood freely flowing from his neck and looked at it in confusion.

How was I going to make it unnoticeable?

I suddenly recalled a conversation that I had previously had with Isaac, about Vampire blood healing a human's wound. I looked down at my wrist and frowned. What I was about to do seemed very strange to me.

I paused momentarily, before shrugging and bringing my wrist up to my mouth. I quickly bit down hard, taking a sharp intake of breath at the sudden searing pain. After remembering that a Vampire's wound heals almost immediately, I brought my bleeding wrist up to the man's mouth. Tilting his head back, I kept my wrist in place, tricking the blood down into his throat. Less than a second later I felt my skin heal and I lowered my hand.

Sure enough, his skin began to heal and within three seconds, his wound was completely unnoticeable and he once again regained consciousness.

The moment he opened his eyes, I pressed him back against the wall and looked deeply into them "You don't remember any of this. Go back to having a drink."

I released him and then saw the blood staining his white shirt.

That was going to be an issue.

I laughed inwardly as I reached forward and ripped his shirt open, the buttons flying off. I raised one eyebrow momentarily in admiration of his figure, before pulling it down his arms and clearing the blood from his neck.

"There we go. Perfect!" I smiled at my work, wiping his blood from around my mouth.

"If anyone asks, you got warm." I informed him.

He nodded before walking out of the small alley and back towards the pub. I turned to follow him, when I felt an immense strength push me back into the small alley.

James stood in front of me, our bodies only centimetres apart. He looked down at me and into my eyes, and I felt my heart beat increasing.

I suddenly had the urge to pull him towards me and begin kissing him, but I quenched that desire as soon as it had happened. I put it down to the sudden increase in my range of emotions due to the unnamed man's blood coursing through my veins.

"Pretty good for your first time, but next time stop when I tell you to."

"How *did* you tell me? I didn't know that Vampires could force messages into people's minds."

"That's because normal Vampires can't do that. Neither can born-Vampires until they turn a human. You see, the Lythia bond is normally used in romantic relationships between the Vampire and the human, so they can read each other's thoughts and communicate telepathically."

*Romantic, huh?* I laughed inwardly.

*Yes.* Came his reply.

Crap. I had forgotten straight away that he could read my thoughts. *How long had he known about this ability..?* I queried, thinking back to my thought processes in his bedroom that morning.

*Lucy, I've known this information since I could first process words.* He chuckled back.

I groaned inwardly. That was *not* fair.

He shrugged and gave me a seductive half smile "Needless to say, your thoughts are very interesting."

"I think we should get back to the others – I've had my breakfast, now let's go." I began walking out from the alley.

"Aww really?" He purred "We were only just getting started."

I turned back to face him and raised an eyebrow, giving him a small smile that made my eyes glitter with humour. "Stop. Let's go back."

He laughed "Alright. We're expecting my brother soon, anyway."

We both began walking back towards the pub and as we neared the door, he quickly moved past me and I felt a slight tap on my backside as he entered the building.

*Did he just...?*

*You're an asshole!* I consciously thought to him, working along the mental connection that he had previously established.

I almost sensed the mischievous grin on his face, and as I entered the booth, I saw that exact expression directed at me.

"Move." I commanded shortly. "You're in my spot." Although I attempted to be serious, he could still sense how humorous the situation appeared to me.

"Why don't you sit on my knee?"

"Can you *not?!*" I asked, pointing to my left, indicating for him to stand up from his seat so that I could resume my previous position within the booth. "Move."

He rolled his eyes "Fine. How about–"

"I swear to god, I will bite you." I interrupted him before he could flirt with me further.

He simply shot me another of his famous grins as I shuffled past. I then narrowed my eyes at him as I sat down.

I turned my eyes to Helena and saw that she had been watching me closely the entire time.

*You two are really hitting it off.* I heard.

"Oh shut up Helena." I laughed.

She frowned. "I didn't say anything."

"Yeah you did! Literally just a second ago."

"No she didn't." Elaine clarified.

*Something's happening...* Elaine added.

"What do you mean 'something's happening'?"

Her face fell. "You heard that?"

"Of course I did – I'm not deaf."

Now James was frowning at me.

"Lucy, she didn't say anything."

"Yes, but I thought it." Elaine interjected. "You're a telepath..." She concluded bluntly.

"Yeah, James showed me that I am."

Out of the corner of my eye, I saw him quickly shake his head. "No, I said that only the two of us share the same 'wavelength' so to speak. You shouldn't be able to read anyone else's thoughts."

"But you can." Elaine added.

"It seems so." Helena frowned.

"I think there is a lot about Lucy that we don't know." Lucien interrupted.

We all turned our heads and Elaine rose from her position beside Helena so that he could take it.

"I'm not sure if Helena told you, but I know why you passed out yesterday."

I shrugged "Surely it was just because there were just so many things going on at once?" I tried to make the situation seem less than it was, but personally, I had been terrified.

"Yeah, and how does that explain the blood that came from your nose? That isn't normal." Helena snapped. I could feel her concern and anxiety from across the table.

Lucien also seemed to notice this, and placed his left arm around her waist in an attempt to comfort her.

"You're right, it isn't at all. This is about you as well Helena." He turned to look at her, pulling her a little closer to him. "First of all, Helena didn't have cancer. Although, I think we all know this, judging by how she reacted towards Isaac's blood."

She appeared confused. "I thought it was. Apparently Vampire blood doesn't heal cancer, it just kills the person suffering."

James shook his head in response "No, it *speeds* the cancer up. The cancer which Isaac believed you to have been suffering from would not have had those effects."

"But do you know what she really had?" I queried, concerned for my sister.

"It wasn't exactly an illness, it was more of a parasite."

"What?" Helena asked, a disgusted, confused look on her face. "A *parasite?!*"

"So did you Lucy. You both became hosts for a single creature. Helena had taken the brunt of its attack, but part of it still dug into you. The Ekimmu-"

I felt James's whole body go rigid beside me, and Elaine seemed to have had almost the same reaction. "-which attacked you was an extremely dangerous force of nature that people die of daily. Isaac was not wrong in assuming that you had cancer, because that is what they look like in medical exams: A poisonous tumour."

"Where is this 'Ekimmu' thing then?!" I asked, concerned.

"They latch themselves on to a person's back originally, as that way they can crawl up the host's spine and into their head." Lucien explained.

I had begun to feel nauseous.

"From there, they infiltrate your thoughts. Ekimmus are very violent, angry creatures and they cause the human they inhabit to share those same traits."

So that's why, after Helena's death, I had felt a rage-filled darkness possess my body: One actually had.

"Also." James interrupted. "I'm not sure if you know this, brother, but they're actually Vampires. As you are aware, not all humans survive the transition between Dhampir and Vampire. So when they die, they become a kind of wraith. Now that wraith can either dissipate, unable to harm anyone, or if they die in a certain malevolent frame of mind then they come back as an Ekimmu."

"This doesn't explain why I passed out." I breathed, attempting to conceal my fear and discomfort.

"It does." Elaine began "Because Helena still has part of the creature attached to her."

Helena's eyes widened and she tried to look over her shoulder, feeling up and down her back, searching for the 'creature'.

"But don't worry." She quickly added "When you transform, the creature has no power over you because you are physically stronger than it."

Elaine returned her gaze to me and continued explaining the situation. "When you and Helena were apart, the Ekimmu could still infiltrate your thoughts, but it was almost unnoticeable. You see, it doesn't just make you angry, it also drains your life-force - Like a Vampire would drink your blood. That's why Helena was dying: She had been affected most by the creature and it had the strength it needed to start draining her."

Out of the corner of my eye I saw Helena look down, her porcelain face becoming paler. I moved my foot against her shin, acquiring her attention. When she looked up I gave her a reassuring smile.

Elaine didn't seem to notice Helena's discomfort and continued talking. "When you arrived at the house, the Ekimmu that still resided within Helena rose to the surface and because of the close proximity between the two of you, your part had gained the strength it needed to begin feeding. It seems that it had a very large appetite causing it to almost completely drain you immediately. This is what caused you to fall unconscious."

Against my better judgement of knowing that I wouldn't find the creature, I lifted my hand up to my back, searching for *something* that was out of place.

"So it's gone now?" I asked weakly.

"It will never truly disappear, but you are now stronger than it."

"I'm not sure about that." I began. "After I had turned, I went completely crazy at James, similar to how I was when I was a human. You said that the Ekimmu causes you to be angry? I think that was what caused it, because every time I felt like that before, I almost *felt* something poking around in my mind."

"That makes sense – That's also why your sister has a slight temper on her too: Although the creature has been subdued, it was still a part of your mind, so its presence will have left a lasting effect."

"It's okay now though, because I have James." I gave him a small smile, but he frowned in response.

"Why does that matter?"

" I told you – Every time I felt the 'darkness' in my mind, your voice destroyed it."

A frown still resided on his face as Elaine responded to my statement.

"You could be right – It has been found that certain types of sound kind of paralyses the Ekimmu. I have only heard about that on very rare occasions as the sounds are unique for each individual. I've also noticed that the more negative feelings that reside in your mind, the stronger the creature becomes. That is why when you have positive experiences and emotions, it is also subdued slightly."

"This is crazy." I muttered.

I knew that 'Your Last Goodbye's music had been powerful, but I had never expected it to literally *ward of monsters.*

"Now we all know what's going on, let's go shopping?" Elaine suggested hopefully, attempting to change the topic as quickly as possible onto a lighter subject.

But my instincts suddenly told me that I should not accept Elaine's proposition.

"No." I spoke clearly, shaking my head "We need to go home."

*Home.* I already referred to the mansion which I had spent a single night in, as home...

But I could not deny it – That place was where I belonged. I had known that from the moment I stepped across the threshold. Although I had died in that building, I had also been given a new, improved way of life, within which I would be guided by one of the men that I had the most respect for in this world, and my twin sister. I knew I would be happy.

"Why–" Elaine began, but I quickly interrupted her.

"I ignored my instincts before. Something is going to happen and I need to be there. I couldn't tell you what. But something is going to happen. Let's go."

The second I entered the building I quickly looked around, expecting havoc to have broken out in the room. Fortunately, I was incorrect and there was nothing out of place.

I frowned as my instincts had never let me down before.

What did they mean?

Was something going to happen?

I decided to try and make myself comfortable in a back corner, next to a small, Victorian style burgundy lamp. But I was unable to be still in my own skin and I sat with my back straight, unable to shake the feeling of dread that was slowly increasing by the minute.

Something was going to happen.

I could *feel* it.

I sat in silence for the following ten minutes, waiting in fearful anticipation of the unknown, oncoming force that had shaken me so deeply to my core.

Elaine sat down beside me and I felt her concerned gaze washing over me.

"Hey Lucy, don't be so stressed. Eternity will be awful if you're constantly on edge."

I shook my head vigorously.

"No. I don't know what or when, but something bad is going to happen." I once again flicked my eyes around the room, looking for any signs of a disturbance.

"Take me for instance." Elaine continued, attempting to draw my attention from the matter at hand. "I'm two hundred and seventy three years old, and if I had been miserable the entire time, my life would have been terrible."

Her statement had the desired effect and I turned to look at her.

"Seriously?"

She nodded.

It had not occurred to me that anyone here could be over the age of thirty, but the truth was quite the contrary – I was probably sharing the same building with some of the oldest creatures in the world. This thought sparked my curiosity.

"How old are James and Lucien?"

"Umm..." She looked to the side as if attempting to recall some information and she chucked. "As their aunt, I really *should* know this! I'm a terrible person...

Oh yeah!

James is one hundred and twenty five, and Lucien recently turned one hundred and twenty. You should have *seen* James's one hundredth! It was hilarious! He hired some strippers to flirt with Marius. They also gave him a lap dance. It was honestly the funniest thing I had seen in my entire life. Oh, my brother-in-law is so uptight!"

I smiled along with her until my mind had processed what she had said.

"Marius is your brother-in-law and James and Lucien are your nephews?"

Her face fell and her eyes took on a steely look of fire.

"Yes." She responded, confirming my suspicions. "Victoria is my sister."

"Bloody hell..." I opened my mouth in an attempt to say something else, but I couldn't find the words so I closed it again, shaking my head.

"But if she comes within one metre of you, I will tear her throat out." She added, not blinking.

Her sudden burst of anger shook me slightly and I didn't understand it.

"But she's your sister." I thought about my relationship with Helena and I knew that I could *never* hurt her, let alone kill her.

"By blood only. She stole my child, killed my husband and took my powers." She shook her head slightly, reliving past terrors.

I was lost for words as she continued with her furious speech.

"She also killed Lucien's familiar and her unborn child. Lucien's child. Victoria killed her own unborn grandson in attempt to gain more power. The *only* reason that myself, Marius, Lucien, and James are not currently buried six feet underground is because she, for some unknown reason, abides by a code. Her morals are twisted, monstrous, poisoned things, yet she refuses to kill us." She grabbed my hands before continuing. "That is why, if she ever tries to lay a finger on you, I will kill her without a second thought."

I was touched by how protective everyone was in this vicinity. They treated me as though they had known me for years and acted as though I was actually a member of their family who they would *die* to protect. To them I wasn't just a girl that they had briefly known for a maximum of two days. I didn't understand it, but I appreciated it more than anything in the world. They made me feel like I truly belonged there. As I thought more about how each and every person I had come into contact with – with the exception of Irina– was ready to fight to protect me, no matter what, I realised that they actually *were* my family. Elaine acted in a very maternal way towards me, possibly because of the loss of her child and because of that, perhaps she felt as though she had to protect me from suffering the same fate? I didn't know the exact reason, but I seemed important to her. I looked around the room at all the other Vampires and I saw how they sat within such a close proximity to one another, laughing, enjoying themselves, in an eternity that could have been filled with misery, loneliness and pain. It was truly wonderful to see.

In my old life, I had always felt as though something was wrong. I never managed to befriend many people and they always turned away or betrayed me. My mind briefly flashed to Alice's pale face, framed by her large, bouncing, blonde curls. I took comfort in knowing that I would never have to see her again, and in one hundred years everyone I had known would have died anyway. Including her.

More memories flashed through my mind of sitting in the public library, tens of books about mythology surrounding me. I had sat with both my headphones in, blasting out music from 'Your Last Goodbye' and in those sweet, treasured moments, I felt as though I belonged.

Elaine smiled at me. "Yeah, you really are our family now, Lucy."

"Are you a telepath too?" I asked, frowning.

She chuckled "No, I can just see the happiness and admiration on your face."

"Oh."

She placed her hand on my arm and smiled again. "You really aren't aware of how much you mean to us. Although I, myself, have only known you for a couple of days, Helena has told me everything about you. That's why, the second I met you personally, I knew you would be a perfect addition to our little family here." She indicated around the room. "We fight for each other and we would all gladly lay down our lives to protect the ones we love." She turned back to me. "And now, you are comfortably positioned within that category. Welcome to the family."

Happy tears formed in the corner of my eyes and I laughed, wiping them away.

"You have no idea how much that means to me, Elaine. Thank you."

She reached forward and hugged me.

"No need to thank me, girl. Anyway I'm not sure if you know this, but you're also a little *more* special than you may realise. If James did in fact turn you, which from everything I have witnessed, that fact is blindingly obvious, then you are his familiar. That means you possess all the powers that he does."

I nodded. "Yeah, James mentioned that. I've learnt that we are impervious to sunlight and we can have children, but that's all I know. Why, what other 'powers' do I have?" I queried, my attention and curiosity well and truly held.

"As a Vampire nerd, this information will really hurt your head." She began. "Born-Vampires have the ability of sorcery. We also physically stop growing at twenty one years, but we can make ourselves look to be a different age than we are."

I nodded, absorbing this new information. I thought back to the idea that I could bear children and I frowned. As I was eighteen I had never really had any maternal thoughts, but now I came to think of it, the ability to have children really seemed like a blessing as I knew, in the future, I would have missed it if I couldn't. Elaine was correct, all of this information betrayed every single thing that I had learnt about Vampires, and it did make me question the accuracy of the knowledge that I had prided myself on having for the past three years.

"So you can really do that? You can use sorcery?"

She shook her head. "Not anymore - Victoria took my powers from me. That is the reason I look older than Lucien and James: I made myself that way because I wanted to appear as the 'ideal' mother for Layla. I thought it would be a little strange for her growing up, having me look like her older sister more than her mother." She sighed. "Although it's pointless now and I am stuck like this forever, because I lost my ability to change my age."

"Layla... It's a pretty name."

She smiled, obviously happy at the conversation focus of her daughter. "It means 'dark night', and Grace, her middle name, means 'beauty': 'Beautiful dark night.' Jackson and I saw it fitting as she was our little 'princess of the night'." Elaine let out a small chuckle, looking down at her hands. "That was what she made us call her. She thought that we were the King and Queen, and she was our little princess." She let out a deep sigh, a painful look entering her eyes. She obviously attempted to keep her spirits up by reminiscing on another, beautiful memory.

"Every full moon she used to run out to the big Oak tree in the garden and climb its branches, getting right to the top. She would then just lie back and look at the starlit sky until she fell asleep, after which her father or myself had to carry her back inside."

I smiled at her again and I was about to say something else when the sound of a beautiful, slow, melodious piano floated around the room.

I turned to see that the members of 'Your Last Goodbye' had taken to their stage, and Damian had begun playing the first notes to 'The Eyes of the Soul'.

When I turned back to Elaine, I saw that her gaze was fixed intently on Damian, and I could see tears welling in her eyes. From what I saw in her mind, this song had always helped her at the times she felt particularly paralysed by her husband's passing, and her daughter's kidnapping. I noticed that she was shaking slightly, tears streaming down her face and I reached forward, hugging her towards me. She began sobbing into my shoulder as I embraced her.

I held her until the tears ceased to wrack her body, and when they had stopped she pulled back from me, giving me a watery smile.

"Thank you Lucy... I think I'm going to go and get some rest. See you later."

I attempted to give her a reassuring smile as I watched her leave the room. The second she had disappeared from my sight, the dread once again descended upon my soul with such force, it momentarily took my breath away.

Something was in the room with me.

I could feel a pair of terrifying eyes fixed upon me but no matter how much I turned in my seat, I could not locate their source. I felt like a small, powerless animal, being watched by a predator that was ready to strike at any moment.

*It is happening.*

The voice that had been silent for almost a full day decided to once again make its presence known.

"I have an announcement that no-one of you will like." James began. I snapped my head up to look at him, and I saw that he was addressing the full crowd of Vampires that were situated in front of him. I frowned at his message, but my eyes widened as he continued. "About our latest guest." Everyone in the room turned, their eyes focussed directly on me.

James looked at me before continuing further. "As you all know, I am a born-Vampire, and through complicated and unexpected circumstances... I turned Lucy. For those of you who have been with us for over a century, you will know that the last time this happened, my mother decided to pay us a visit. There were casualties and many of them, but this time we are not losing a single soul. Victoria is coming. We are going to fight, and this time we're going to win."

From the moment he had uttered the word 'Victoria', there had been many fearful mutterings from around the room, and I had received a number of varying looks, ranging from slight discomfort, through to sheer horror.

I realised that some of the Vampires in this crowd would only have joined the coven *after* Victoria's previous attack, meaning that they would have learned of her wrath through stories.

"This time we are burying *her*, not members of our family. Training begins in an hour in the basement. Victoria is very powerful: She has killed and stolen the powers of many, and with their blood on her hands she will try and destroy each and every one of you who stands between her and Lucy. I am so sorry about having to involve you all in this, I really am, but no-one is safe until she is dead."

SOPHIE PETFORD

Everyone had fallen silent through the duration of James's speech and now that he had finished, a slow, definite clap was heard around the room.

*IT IS HAPPENING!*

Screamed the voice in my head.

Oh my god. It was here. The deadly threat that I had been terrified of the past hour was here.

I saw everyone turning in their seats in all directions, attempting to find the source of the noise.

"Well well well. James, *darling*, that is no way to speak about your mother!"

Everyone turned their heads to the right, following the voice, as a tall woman, dressed in a black fitted dress with long, crimson hair entered the room, a malicious smile painted on her blood red lips.

She gazed intently at James as she continued walking slowly into the room, the sound of her high heels clicking against the wooden floor.

She tore her eyes away from him and slowly looked around the room until she found me.

When her eyes connected with mine, her smile widened, revealing unnaturally long, pointed canines.

"Lucy..." She almost hissed with excitement. The second she uttered my name, her irises shone a magnificent, strong red.

I didn't need to be told that this woman was in fact James's mother, as I felt the immense power radiating from her pale skin.

"Victoria." I breathed.

Her grin became even wider, stretching unnaturally up her cheeks, contorting her face into a monstrous image. Her teeth had become sharpened, deadly weapons and her canines had elongated to hang below her lower lip. The white of her eyes had also turned a deathly black, her red irises remaining. Black lines, similar to cracks, crawled out from the side of her eyes, ending at her cheeks.

133

Her terrifying, unnatural, horrifying image was the last thing I saw before I was plunged into darkness.

# CHAPTER EIGHT

F*ive months previously...*
Bright flood lights flashed around the spacious, high ceilinged arena and the sound of guitars screaming in perfect agony could be heard, providing life to the crowd only metres away.

I gazed around in wonder at the way in which the members of this heavy rock band positioned themselves, and how naturally they all fell into their roles; how the two guitarists' skin seemed to be almost melded to their instruments, becoming one with them; how the singer's voice sounded like the that of an angel's, combined with the fiery passion of a demon, and how the long haired, shirtless drummer beat the hell out of his kit: Stamping on the pedal of his bass as if crushing those who had ever pushed him down, and abusing the rest of the equipment, defying everyone who had ever told him that he couldn't make something of himself by simply 'hitting a few pieces of plastic'. Then there was Benjamin who played a slow beat on his bass guitar. At first his contribution may not have seemed as important as the other instruments, due to the fact that he had only four strings to tell his story. But upon closer inspection it is found that he is the backbone to the band. Without him, any song they perform is hollow and empty, but with it, the members of 'Your Last Goodbye' made something that was a dark, beautiful kind of magic. A magic that somehow reached hundreds of thousands of people on a personal level, shaking them to their very core, raising them from a sleep they never knew themselves to be within and providing *life* to people who didn't know that they weren't living.

This band was unnatural, inhuman, and created music that could be the anthem to the fiery depths of hell itself: Raising the dead, damning the sinners and becoming a saviour to those most in need.

Just as suddenly as the song had begun, it came to an end. But the sounds of the guitars were almost immediately replaced by the screaming and cheering of the leather clad, black haired crowd that were the members of their army.

"Thank you everybody! We have been 'Your Last Goodbye'! Goodnight London!" James shouted into his microphone, raising his left hand in a farewell gesture, before leaving the stage with his fellow band members in tow.

"That was *amazing!*" My mother yelled, jumping giddily, her eyes filled with excitement.

"I told you!" I replied, the same gleam present within my own two eyes, that were lined with heavy, dark make-up.

"Everyone in there was also exactly like you." She gestured towards my outfit. "I thought you were alone in your leather and eyeliner."

I laughed, shaking my head. "Not at all." I pointed back into the arena that we had just exited. "Those people in there: I don't know even a hundredth of them, but I know we are all the same. They're like my family."

She raised an eyebrow in a way that suggested I was slightly insane, but she smiled anyway. This was *my* night, my *perfect* night. My mother had brought me here as a surprise for my eighteenth birthday, and I had spent the entire evening absorbing the sounds of their instruments and singing along with the other members of the crowd.

"Holy crap! Lucy, look!" Her face had fallen and she pointed behind me to the left of the building. I turned to follow her gaze and I almost fainted.

"No... that isn't..."

"IT IS! GET YOUR ASS OVER THERE RIGHT NOW!"

My mother had managed to spot, with her eagle eyesight, the front of a red and black bus... 'Your Last Goodbye's tour bus... If she had not pointed it out, I would never have even noticed the vehicle, as around only an eighth of it wasn't concealed by shadows.

I stood frozen in place, my eyes fixed upon the metal machine that transported the people I admired the most, around the world, enabling them to spread their music and bring light to more people's lives.

"Lucy! What are you *doing?!* Get over there!"

"I–" My tongue was tied and I remained attached to my spot on the concrete, not blinking, not believing what my eyes were showing me.

My mother quickly moved behind me and shoved me gently in the direction of the vehicle, shaking me from my shocked state, and I slowly began stumbling forward.

"I'll meet you at the car later Lucy!" She shouted after me.

Once I had gained full control of my legs, I began walking quicker, a shocked smile slowly forming on my lips as I realised the reality of the situation. I then broke into a run and upon reaching the wall of the arena, I leant back against it, breathing heavily in anticipation of the event that was about to occur.

It seemed that no-one else had managed to find the almost fully concealed vehicle, making the moment appear as if it was a dream. If it had in fact been a dream, I wouldn't have cared – As long as I could remember that dream for the rest of my life, I would have been happy.

I closed my eyes and leant my head against the cool brickwork. *This is actually happening.* I thought to myself. *I'm going to meet them...*I couldn't believe my luck that evening and as I stood there, I remembered the letter in the front pocket of my jeans. I quickly pulled it free and clutched it to my chest. My breathing rapidly increased as the moment came closer and closer and the second that I felt as though I was about to faint, I heard a door open to my left.

My heart skipped a beat and my breath caught in my throat.

*Oh my God.*

I heard him before I saw him...

*James Killoran.*

"Right! As he suggested, we're gonna' do shots until the sun comes up!" He laughed with the other members of his band. As he turned his head in the direction of his tour bus, he almost walked right into me.

"Oh sorry. I didn't see you."

He looked down at me, and my breathing still had not returned to a normal pace.

He gave me a warming smile and spoke again. "Hi, are you alright?"

I nodded, unable to speak a word as I held out the letter in my quivering hand.

The other men had walked past us and had already boarded the bus, as James stood with me.

He gently took the slightly crumpled paper from me and smiled. "Thank you."

He then turned and followed the others in the direction of the bus, jogging up the steps.

I turned, still completely numb by the encounter and I started to walk slowly back towards my mother's car.

I couldn't believe it... I had met him...

My mind flashed back to his piercing blue eyes as I felt a small tap on my shoulder. Naturally, I turned to see who had requested my attention, and my eyes widened once more as I saw that it was *him.*

"Hey, sorry about that. I was just telling Simon to wait." He gave me another one of his perfect, closed mouthed–smiles that made his eyes glisten.

"Anyway," He pulled the letter from the inside pocket of his high collared leather jacket and held it up to me. "I see that you have something for me."

My blood turned to ice as I realised that he was about to open and read the letter in *front* of me...

I had written it in the faintest hope that I would be able to give it him as he walked passed me, surrounded by masses of other fans. But now he was talking to *me* and me alone, and he was reading it *in front of me.*

I watched his face closely as he took in the words, scrawled across the paper in my messy handwriting.

Once he had finished reading it, he folded it up, proceeding to place it back in his inside pocket. Without saying a word, he reached down and pulled me into a tight hug.

My entire body appeared to crumble and I felt myself fall unconscious.


(James)

Her entire figure crumpled in my arms and I quickly pulled back, attempting to stand her upright. That was when I saw it... The blood flowing from her nose.

I immediately picked her up and ran back to the bus, laying her down on the sofa.

Everyone had already begun making their way towards me, having heard my rushed entrance.

Chris frowned "What's going on? Why'd you bring a human on here?"

Damian pushed forward and stood next to her. "She's bleeding... What the hell happened James?!"

I raised my hands in a defensive motion. "Don't ask me. I didn't do anything."

Something was wrong.

"Wait... can you hear that?" I asked, silencing the rest of them with a raised finger.

"Hear what?" Josh asked.

"Exactly..." Lucy didn't have a heat beat.

A small, weak thud was heard. It seemed that she was still alive, but only barely.

"She's dying..."

Without thinking, I bit open my wrist and placed it to her lips, forcing my blood down her throat in an attempt to revive her.

Everyone recoiled in shock.

"James! What are you *doing?!*" Ben yelled.

"None of you were doing anything and *look* at her! It's Helena's sister!"

I felt them lean closer towards her unconscious figure, moments later withdrawing in understanding.

"Oh."

"How did we not see that?"

"You can see the similarity..."

"Can you guys *shut up?!*" I snapped, placing my fingers to her neck to check for a pulse. When I felt it increase in speed, I let out a sigh of relief, slumping down on the sofa at her feet.

"Well that was interesting." Chris broke the silence. "Is she joining us for a pint, or are we releasing her back into the wild?"

I quietly looked over her features, frowning. She really did bear resemblance to her sister. "Give her a few more minutes. She has my blood in her system so I want to check that she's okay first. I know she only fainted, but still."

Ben chuckled "Is she really that much of a die-hard fan?"

Nodding, I looked up at him. "Yeah, it seems so."

I returned my gaze to Lucy's face, my eyebrows furrowed as I remembered the contents of her letter.

To this day, it still amazed me that we could touch people's lives so deeply and have them rely on us so much... I couldn't believe that we could actually bring happiness to those who were otherwise lost...

Suddenly, she began coughing and I immediately jumped up, pulling her into a sitting position. Her coughing became heavier by the second and it appeared that she was still unconscious, even through this fit of aggressive, body quaking chokes.

She then began coughing up blood.

By the smell of it, I could tell that it was human blood, *not* my own that she had just ingested.

Something was very, *very* wrong: My blood had never failed in curing a human before.

She coughed three more times before collapsing back onto the soft cushions, the flow of blood from her mouth ceasing.

We all stood there, frozen in shock at her unmoving figure.

"What the hell is going on?!" Ben demanded.

I opened my mouth to reply, but I shut it again, my eyes taking on a solemn, terrified look.

Her heartbeat had once again stopped. But this time, she had died with *my* blood in her system...

"Oh my god." I breathed.

"James..." Damian began.

"I KNOW!" I roared back in response, snapping my head round to face him.

Unperturbed by my aggressive action, he continued.

"She's a Dhampir now... your Dhampir..."

"I SAID I KNOW!" I yelled once again, standing upright. I attempted to control the shivers of fear, anger, and confusion that flooded through my system. Then, in as calm a voice that I could manage, I asked "What am I going to do..?"

Sensing my distress, Damian walked closer to me.

"We take her away from here." He indicated out of the windows, toward the sounds of the shouting fans that were still within our earshot. "We get her away from the humans and we take her to the woods or an isolated field or something: Somewhere quiet where we can think. Then you call Isaac, as he'll know what to do. Needless to say, we can't stay here."

I nodded, latching on to the small shred of a plan that we had in place. Now that I had a set of instructions to follow, everything else was just white noise. I just had to focus on getting out of there.

I turned and took Simon's position at the wheel.

"I know exactly where to go." I muttered, positioning myself within the seat.

"Aren't we going to find the woman she arrived with?" He queried in his strong, Scottish accent.

"Good point." I turned my head away from the windscreen and shouted back into the bus. "Can someone go and find the woman who Lucy came with? From what Helena has said, it was her mother."

"I got it." Josh replied, jumping down the steps and jogging across the concrete of the car park.


A few minutes later, he returned with a middle aged woman with long, straight, brown hair and hazel eyes. I immediately recognised her as the woman who was with Lucy in the crowd, earlier that evening.

"Hi." She smiled awkwardly at me as she entered the bus. "Um, what am I doing here?"

When I responded with a grim facial expression, her smile dropped and her eyes took on a protective, aggressive look. "Where's my daughter?" She asked calmly, but I could hear the increase in her heart rate.

Without saying a word, I looked back into the vehicle, gesturing with my head.

I heard her begin shouting, a terrified, exasperated tone to her voice. "What have you done to her?!"

Before any of the others could respond, I quickly put the bus into reverse and turned it round, before speeding out of the main exit.

This sudden movement had appeared to take her off guard, as she yelped in response to my acceleration.

I could hear Josh commanding her to 'go to sleep', which was extremely helpful as the last thing I needed was Lucy's mother complicating matters further.

Moments later, Damian walked through to the head of the bus to join me.

"Where are we headed?"

"To a forest with *no* distractions." I replied shortly, fixing my eyes on the darkened road.

Within twenty minutes we had arrived at our destination.

I had not experienced a single moment of peace the entire journey, as my mind was tortured with the incident that had occurred that evening:

Lucy had died with my blood in her system...

She would be my familiar...

We would share the Lythia bond...

I didn't even really know this girl, but I was to be forever linked with her. My one chance at ever having my own children had been spent on her...

Also, Victoria would be coming for her.

Fear had kept me alert the entire journey and my eyes had been fixed on the road that gradually turned from one of smooth tarmac, to a patchy uneven surface, and finally, to dirt.

I stopped when I could no longer fit the bus between the tall trees that loomed ominously over the vehicle, filling me with a deep sense of dread.

Something bad was going to happen... I could *feel* it.


I stood and returned to my seated position at Lucy's feet, looking round at the other men, a fearful -but controlled- expression on my face.

"What now?" I asked, breaking the silence.

Damian opened his mouth to speak but I held up a hand, silencing him.

*Crunch*

I froze.

Something was in the forest with us.

*Crunch*

It was louder this time, the dry leaves telling of another creature within the darkness.

*Crunch*

My eyes widened as I heard the sound directly outside the wall of the bus. I slowly leant against metal, placing my ear up to it.

I could almost *feel* the other creature that was mere metres away from me.

I did not scare easily, but whatever was on the other side of that wall had me terrified: It radiated power and shook me to my very core as I could feel the darkness which inhabited that demon.

Suddenly there was a knock on the door: A slow, light, but firm knock that sounded three times.

We all snapped our necks round to the source of the sound, our eyes fixed upon the door. Slowly and hesitantly, I rose from my feet and walked towards it.

With each step, the darkness seemed to worm its way further into my mind, seeking out my fear and exploiting it.

Although by the time I reached the door I felt as though I was suffocating in terror, I still reached towards the handle.

I grabbed the cool, thin piece metal firmly and held it in my hand for a few moments before I slowly turned it, opening the door to reveal the horror that waited on the other side.

"James, darling! Long time no see. I sense you have a present for me?"

I stood there in numbed horror as my mother forced her way onto the bus, her blood red hair framing her malicious expression. Even as she passed me the touch of her fingertips burnt my skin, blistering immediately due to the dark power that radiated from her demonic form.

Her ruby eyes lit up as she saw Lucy's unconscious figure, and with the elegance of a hunting cat, she crossed the length of the bus to stand by her side.

Victoria turned to look at me as she pointed a perfectly manicured claw at Lucy's pale face.

"Why this girl?"

"I don't know what you're talking about." I choked out, fear still clogging my throat.

"Do not be rude James." She scolded me. "I asked, why her?" In the blink of an eye, her expression had changed from one of playful curiosity to anger, and she brought her right hand up, grabbing the air in front of her with a death-like hold.

I felt the skin around my neck tighten as she cut off my oxygen. I felt frantically around my throat, trying to free myself from her grasp.

She then released me and I immediately doubled over, coughing.

"Now are you going to answer me?" She asked, her hand on her hip and an impatient expression on her face.

"She was dying! I don't know why."

"And your blood did not heal her?" She once again turned her gaze back to Lucy's face. "How curious."

145

Victoria then quickly turned back to me. "Either way, you know that I am going to have to kill her, don't you?"

"Why?" I asked " Why do you always have to kill?"

My mother flashed me a wide, toothy grin. "Because, my dear son, power is the most important thing in this world."

"You have enough!"

She laughed. "Oh, you have much to learn! Don't you see? You can *never* have enough power."

I shook my head at her in despair.

"You have power, but you have no-one."

Another smile crossed her face and she sighed in a mocking fashion. "Emotions such as compassion and love make you weak! No, the friendships I have are with people who are useful to me: Pawns in my little game. In time you will learn this."

"No, those emotions don't make you weak. What the hell do you live for mother?!"

"Power." She said shortly, as if discussing the matter with an infant.

"But why?" I asked, desperate for an answer. Victoria had once been a caring, loving wife and mother, but that woman had abandoned me at the age of fifteen.

"Stop acting like a child." She snapped. "And let's get down to business – oh hello. Who's this?" She turned to Lucy's mother and tilted her head.

When I didn't reply, she looked between the two unconscious women.

"They look similar... Judging by her age, my guess is that the girl is her daughter? Well perhaps, mother to mother, *she* will listen to me."

Victoria shot forward and seized her by the side of her head. After muttering a couple of words, Lucy's mother took a deep intake of breath, looking around her wildly.

"Who are you?" She asked, trying to back away from Victoria. She was then flashed a big, perfect smile.

"Hello dear, my name is Victoria and, like yourself, I am a mother. My son is not giving me any useful information–" She snapped her head round and shot me an fiery glare, before returning her gaze to the woman in front of her. "and your daughter is obviously fast asleep, so I was wondering if you could tell me a little about what she is?"

She frowned. "What do you mean *what* she is? She is my daughter and she's called Lucy. I have no idea where we are and why I am here, but can we just leave now?"

She looked questioningly at me and I then saw my mother's expression change to one of boredom.

Standing back and looking at this woman, she sighed "You really aren't of any use to me." With one fluid motion, she leant down, grabbed the side of her head between her hands and twisted it one hundred and eighty degrees. The crack of Lucy's mother's broken neck shot through the silence within the bus, the sound of her heartbeat ending immediately.

"No!" I ran forward but Victoria immediately spun around, her eyes glowing a bright red. She once again outstretched her hand, but this time her palm was facing me and no matter how hard I struggled against her, I was unable to move even an inch.

Lucy suddenly began to stir and I looked between her and the lifeless body of her mother. I saw her look of confusion turn to one of immense despair.

"Where am I? Wait– mum? What are you doing– MUM!" She launched herself off the sofa and down at the ground in front of her mother's disfigured, crumpled body.

She frantically grabbed her cheeks, moving her face towards her, but as the lifeless skull rolled in her hands she let out a sob.

"Mum... no– Please! Wake up!" Lucy then removed her hands from her mother's head and began pulling at her arm, begging her to show some sign of life. "Please...Not you too..." She collapsed against the broken body, wrapping her arms around it. "Wake up! Don't leave me..."

She continued to beg for the empty corpse to regain its life, but to no avail, and she progressed to sob into its cold arms.

"Oh how pitiful." Victoria commented, obviously bored with the situation.

Lucy slowly turned her head in the direction of my mother, tears lining her face.

"What?" She whispered.

"She's dead darling. Get over it."

"But..." She looked to the broken corpse on the ground and then back at Victoria. "She's my mother."

"Yes, I gathered that by your incessant whining."

"Wh-what is wrong with you?"

"Apparently I'm evil." She shrugged. "That's why I found it so easy to just snap little mummy's neck here."

Lucy's eyes widened in disbelief. "You did this?"

"Yes, that is what I-"

Before she could utter another word Lucy had launched herself up from the ground, towards my mother's waist, in an attempt to tackle her to floor.

She merely took one step back from her attacker and with the flick of an arm, she threw Lucy across the bus into the wall.

She let out a startled shriek as she made contact with the hard material and fell to the floor.

Within seconds, Lucy had righted herself and once again charged at my mother, unperturbed by her deflection.

But this time, as she made contact, Victoria shot out a hand and grabbed Lucy's heart within her chest.

My mother's attention had seemingly been averted from the rest of us and we ran towards her.

"Ah ah ah." She warned. "In my hand, I have little Lucy's heart." For dramatic effect, she squeezed lightly and Lucy let out a pained yelp. "So I wouldn't rush me if I were you."

I approached my mother with both my palms outstretched, treading very carefully.

"Mother... please..."

"Oh don't tell me you already care for this pathetic creature?"

"She is another person! Of course I care!"

"Caring makes you weak." She retorted, a disgusted look on her face. As I saw her arm tense, about to rip Lucy's heart from her chest, I sensed a change in her decision and she released her.

Lucy fell to the ground, clutching her chest. Kneeling beside her, I placed a hand on her back as she steadied her breathing. I cast my eyes up to my mother, confused as to why she had changed her mind, and concerned as to what she had changed it to.

"I've had a better idea." Victoria informed me, a malicious smile stretching across her face. She proceeded to kneel down and grab Lucy by the neck, walking swiftly over to a wall and slamming her skull against the metal.

Lucy let out a small whimper before falling unconscious.

"Pathetic." Victoria muttered, once again shoving her hand into her chest.

I jumped forward in an attempt to assist Lucy but once again my mother stopped me. "Oh don't worry, I'm not going to kill her: I have something better in mind."

I frowned at her decision to spare her life, as I had the idea that it wasn't without painful consequence.

Victoria muttered a long incantation, her eyes closed as her grip was still strong around Lucy's heart.

Moments later, she removed her hand and Lucy fell to the ground beside the broken corpse of her mother.

"There we go. Sorted. She's a human again now with new memories, so she won't have remembered any of this."

Lucy's heart beat once again sounded around the interior of the bus, even stronger than before.

I frowned and eyed my mother with suspicion as she knelt down next to the body of Lucy's mother and wiped her hand on her shirt, cleaning it free of blood.

When Victoria rose, she gave me a wide smile. "Shouldn't you be thanking me?"

"No because with you, there's always a catch."

"No catch. Lucy's human -in a sense- and she has no memory of today. What else do you want?"

As I opened my mouth to reply, she added something else with a wide, malicious grin.

"But her mother *is* dead and I can't change that -not that I'd want to anyway- but she is. So I've taken your advice, son." She walked slowly towards me, her hands joined behind her back. "You said that I was incapable of caring for another person, yes?"

I didn't reply as I waited for her to continue.

"So I've decided that, because I'm bored at home anyway, I should look after Lucy. Obviously not looking like this. No no, she wouldn't recognise me."

I was suddenly becoming aware of what she was suggesting. "No."

"Oh yes. I will remove your memories from today, so you don't recall this dreadful incident of losing your one and only chance of having a familiar." She shot a look down to the broken body on the floor "Take this woman with you, will you? - I really cannot be bothered to bury her in the forest. Just leave her in the morgue in the basement. She also won't begin to rot as none of my victims ever do, so you won't have to be concerned with the smell. I'll also make you forget about her, as I wouldn't want you telling Helena that I killed her mother." Her eyes then turned to Lucy's unconscious figure. "But yes, I will take Lucy home. Then we will laugh together and talk about boys, or whatever teenage girls do, until she decides to move out in a couple of years. But she will be none the wiser, because I will look like this."

As I stared on in horror, I saw my mother's hair beginning to turn brown, and her eyes lost their terrifying red glow. As the seconds progressed, the features of her face had also changed and within the minute, she was completely unrecognisable. Stood before me was an identical copy of the woman she had murdered only minutes previously.

"Now." She began, looking down at her new body before resuming eye contact with me. "Let's see how well I can care for little Lucy, shall we?"

# CHAPTER NINE

P *resent day*
  I awoke abruptly and flashed my eyes around the room, attempting to learn something of my location. I was unable to gather any information as the only thing that filled my vision was a pitch black, inky darkness. Within the darkness I fell to my knees and closed my eyes, absorbing all of the events that had recently been forced into my mind.

When my eyes re-opened, they did so with a burning fire that filled my mind and I stared hard into the shadows. Even though I could not see anything, I could *sense* her: The monster that had murdered my mother.

"Show yourself!" I roared into the silence, my voice echoing around the walls.

Although she had murdered hundreds of people -including my mother- I did not fear her in the slightest: The adrenaline that burnt through my body had given me a newfound dark strength that, I knew, would give me the power to destroy her.

Victoria's mocking laughter sounded around the room, seeming to come from all directions so I was unable to pinpoint her location.

"Oh *dear*." She began, followed by a sharp snap of her fingers. A dim, red tinted light filled the room and once again, her form took on a monstrous, grotesque appearance as her features contorted and twisted in unnatural ways; her  sly, cunning smile stretched up almost to her cheekbones, revealing rows upon rows of pointed, jagged fangs, coupled with a long, darting, thick, black, forked tongue; her red painted nails stretched into inch long claws, ending up as pointed weapons, used for tearing the life out of her enemies; her once flawless, porcelain skin had become infected with an inky black tint, beginning from around her eyes and proceeding to slowly crawl across her flesh. Once her transformation was complete, she grinned at me, exposing the sheer horror of her terrifying jaws and said "Here I am."

I quickly launched myself across the room at her, but before I made contact, she had moved.

Anticipating some form of resistance, I landed on all fours and snapped my head round, my sharp fangs exposed.

"YOU MURDERED HER!" I screamed, following Victoria's fast moving figure with my hunter's eyes. She appeared to be pacing quickly in front of me, mocking me, taunting me, pushing me to make the next move.

"Yes. I did." She replied with a cruel lack of compassion. "She was weak. Just like you."

I let out an angered shriek and she laughed again, taunting me further.

"You really *are* weak! You were powerless to save her then and even now, you are unable to avenge her death. You pathetic little–"

This time I made contact with her body.

I sunk my teeth deep into her forearm and a second before I swallowed her blood from the wound I had just created, I quickly spat it out, remembering the lethal qualities that it possessed.

She slapped me across the side of the face and sent me flying towards a wall, but once again, I had anticipated her response and I landed on my feet.

"You really are a little pest, aren't you? I should have killed you when I had the chance." She grumbled, wiping the blood from her arm and watching, moments later, as the wound healed itself.

"Well you didn't." I snapped. "And you're wrong: I. Am. Not. WEAK!" I roared at her.

"Temper temper." She scolded me. Her eyes suddenly flashed to mine and with that movement, she brought her right hand up and clutched the air in front of her, tightening her invisible grip around my throat.

I didn't let myself scream from the pain. Instead I let it fuel my rage, and I took two steps forward before collapsing to my knees. Even in that position, I still shuffled towards her, dragging myself along the floor by my nails, tearing them to shreds in the process.

I would kill this woman if it was the last thing I did.

"...Kill...you..." I managed to croak through her death grip. I quickly felt her hold tighten and I heard a *snap* come from my neck.

That was the moment when I would have screamed, but I was unable to release any type of sound as my throat had been well and truly crushed.

"Now you're quiet..." She began, walking forwards. I felt myself sliding back across the floor, slowly at first, but then quicker as Victoria increased her pace towards me. A moment later I felt the back of my skull shatter as I was thrown against the wall and lifted three feet off the ground.

I had felt my throat and skull immediately begin to heal as she held me there, but for good measure, she slammed me once more against the hard stone and tightened her grip further on my throat, crushing it once again.

"I am going to kill you, Lucy." She loosened her grip slightly on my neck, ensuring that I could breathe enough to not fall unconscious: She wanted me to hear her plan of how she was to end my life.

"I am going to tear you apart, limb from limb. I'm going to force myself into your mind, finding the weakest, lowest moments of your pathetic life, and I will fill your mind with them, tearing down each and every defence you have painstakingly built up over time; I will show you the crumpled, burnt, crushed, dismembered body of your father; the twisted, disfigured image of your mother, showing you the fear that I induced within her moments before tearing her life away; I will force every feeling of burning hatred and anger, every crushing sense of self doubt and despair that you have ever endured, into your soul. I will remind you of every time you have felt alone... That is how you will die: Being torn apart from both the inside and the outside. I am going to make you wish that you had never been born, I am going to eradicate *every* single moment of happiness from your life, and finally, when your soul and body alike bleeds for a sweet release, *that* is when I will kill you."

She walked closer to me and I immediately felt her dark tendrils entering my mind. Although I had almost fallen unconscious due to the pain and lack of oxygen, I was still able to exercise my willpower and I forced up thick, barbed walls around my mind, blocking her out.

For now.

I felt her withdraw from my mind and focus more on my body.

She raised her second hand and stretched out a clawed finger. At the same time I felt a burning, searing pain in my right palm and I looked down at my hand, turning it face up. I could see a long, thick gash forming, her claw ripping open my skin as though it was nothing. It held no resistance against her razor sharp weapons that were purely structured to tear flesh apart.

Once the deep gash had formed from the top of my wrist to just beneath the joint of my smallest finger, the burning stopped. Almost immediately, the sensation returned, this time from the opposite side of my hand, forming a bloody 'X' on my palm.

I pushed against the broken bones in my throat in an attempt to let out a piercing scream, as I looked down and torturously felt the triangle layers of my skin slowly being torn back to reveal the red, raw, bloody flesh beneath.

Although my throat was healing as time progressed, my hand was not giving me a single moment of release as Victoria had obviously set it in an un-healing state, forcing me to watch as she continued peeling back the skin until a bloody square of exposed flesh was revealed.

Her mutated mouth opened wide and from the end of her forked tongue, and unidentifiable black creature shot out and landed on the floor.

When I initially looked at the ground, I couldn't make out what it was as it had fallen beneath a chair, but as it scuttled out and was exposed to the light, I saw the horror that Victoria had just released: It was an eight legged, deathly black, red eyed, large fanged spider that appeared to be sneering in content at the blood dripping from my hand.

It quickly made its way towards me, its hairy limbs moving in a perfect, synchronised pace as it neared my broken body.

Without breaking pace, it turned and crawled up the wall, proceeding to launch itself from the stone and land on the back of my head, digging its claws into my hair and flesh. As it made its way along my shoulders and down my right arm, I felt an itching, burning pain along each inch of skin that it travelled across. The creature then slowed its pace as it walked beneath the sleeve of my leather jacket and I could feel its monstrous form expanding. Finally, when the horrifyingly disgusting arachnid stepped out into my sight, it looked up at me, letting me absorb its revolting appearance; every strand of its coarse hair; the blackness of its uneven flesh; the blood red eyes that looked deep into my soul, and finally the teeth: The massive fangs that I had felt dragging along my skin as it forced its way across my body. It seemed aware of exactly how much terror it was inducing within my heart because it continued to keep eye contact with me as it placed its first dirty, infection ridden claw into the open wound of my hand.

In that second my neck had healed entirely as Victoria's attention had been averted to the vile creature that currently resided on my palm. A blood-curdling scream ripped out of my throat as I felt what appeared to be an acid covered, sharp claw digging into my exposed flesh.

Not averting its eyes from mine, the unnatural arachnid forced its foot deeper into my red, raw, bleeding flesh. My scream turned to a louder howl as its other seven legs joined it.

"Now, my pretty..." Victoria hissed. "*Dig.*"

Following her instructive cue, the spider began hungrily and mercilessly burrowing into my flesh.

To halt my screaming, Victoria once again crushed my throat. Tears of pure agony fell from my eyes as I was powerless to stop the creature's ceaseless attacks on my exposed flesh.

From the beginning, Victoria had ensured that my left hand was restrained and twisted against the wall behind me, but my legs thrashed wildly against the excruciatingly torturous moving fire that was continuing to burrow within my hand.

My vision became hazy due to the intense agony that emanated from my hand, but I noticed that Victoria was distracted as I felt her grip loosen on my throat and left arm, allowing them to heal once more. I slowly flexed the fingers of my left hand and in that moment, the torturous pain somehow managed to fuel my rage and with one loud, powerful scream, I brought my left hand up and a large wave of pure power surged from my palm. The immense gust knocked her off her feet and into the wall, momentarily averting her attention from the spider.

I fell to the ground on my hands and knees, yelping as I landed on the open wound.

I suddenly began the feel my skin start to heal...

With the spider still inside my hand.

Gritting my teeth against the pain, I brought my left hand across and began burrowing through my own flesh, attempting to remove the poisoned creature that laid beneath it. When I felt that I could no longer handle the pain, my fingers closed around a long, black leg. I pulled on it with all my strength and slowly, the thrashing, hissing, spitting arachnid emerged from my destroyed flesh.

With an exhausted thrust of power, I launched it across the room where it crashed into the wall beside its master and fell limp to the ground.

As I triumphantly sensed the life disappear from that monstrosity, I saw Victoria slowly rise from the ground, her spine twisted at a grotesque angle, coupled with her shattered shoulder blade that jutted out unevenly from her bloodied, poisoned flesh.

She no longer smiled.

Instead, her eyes had taken on a horrifying blaze of fire, and even after every single moment of pain she had just forced me to endure, her gaze invoked a fresh wave of fear within me. But now my fear had turned to adrenalin and I shot up from the ground and raced across the room and out of the door before Victoria could catch me.

But I heard her chasing me, the cracking of her shattered bones as loud as gun shots as they attempted to heal, ricocheting around the dark, wooden corridors of the building that she pursued me through.

*Where am I?!* I screamed in my mind as I continued racing down the unknown hallways.

As if in response to my terrified question, moments later I found myself right in the front room of the mansion.

I noticed that each and every Vampire in the room was unconscious, sprawled across the ground in the darkness. I scoured their faces in search of either Helena or James and when my eyes finally rested upon his pale face, I bolted towards him.

"James!" I shouted.

When he didn't respond, I grabbed him roughly by the shoulders, sat him upright, and shook him profusely.

"James, wake up!" I half shouted, half begged, as I looked around me, fearful of Victoria's return.

I released him and froze as I sensed another presence within the room. Focussing all my power to my sense of hearing, I sat motionless in an attempt to make out any sound that would give me an idea as to where this other creature was.

A second later, I heard a small *thud* and I immediately spun round, launching myself at the creature, my right hand on its neck, my fangs bared, ready to tear its throat out.

"Helena?!" I shrieked.

"Lucy!"

I quickly released her and retracted my fangs, sitting back upright and wrapping my arms around her.

"How are you awake?!" I asked, adrenaline still coursing through my system.

"I don't know!" She replied, shaking her head rapidly, appearing extremely flustered. "I heard you screaming for James."

Just then, as if on cue, James awoke and ran across the wooden floor and threw himself at me, wrapping his arms around my waist, pushing us both to the ground.

"You're alive!" He breathed, his head furrowed into my shoulder. "Oh my god, you're alive." He repeated, pushing on my back and pressing me closer to him, fearful of letting me go and losing me again.

"She certainly is." Came an angered, muffled voice from the doorway.

Victoria snapped her fingers and the entire room lit up, the red tint returning.

Her bones had only just managed to mend themselves and her once flattering, figure hugging dress was now torn in numerous places, being reduced to a bloody rag that only partially covered her blackened flesh.

She had remained in her grotesque, disfigured Vampiric form as she breathed heavily, her once sleek hair having become matted with blood and sweat, falling over her face in stringy strands.

Despite her obvious fury, her monstrous face once again held a disturbing smile. "But not for long."

With the last word she ran over to me and seized me by the throat.

Except she didn't, as before she was anywhere near me James had stood upright, a fiery look in his eyes and he raced across the room, throwing himself at her grotesque body, barging her into the stone wall.

She fell crumpled to the ground but as she attempted to rise again, I twisted my hand in a swift movement and snapped her leg backwards, shattering the bone, causing her to let out a startled yell as she once again fell to the ground.

She was obviously becoming weaker as time progressed and I continued breaking each individual bone, my eyes fixed upon her ruby irises, causing her ribs to jut out through the rips in the torso of her dress.

"She is new! How is she so strong?!" Victoria commanded, spitting out blood.

James glared at her with a look of pure disgust and returned to my side.

"You've been in her mind, Victoria... you know *just* how strong she is."

He then slowly walked over to her, continuing his speech.

"She has lost her father." *Step.*

"You murdered her mother." *Step.*

"She thought she lost her sister." *Step.*

"She was haunted, nightly, by the horrors that you undoubtedly placed there." *Step.*

He continued until he was within one metre of her, where he crouched down in front of her broken form.

"You made her life hell. You ripped away her happiness. You threatened her life. After all this do you not think that this girl has gained the emotional and physical power to take. You. Down." He spat the final words at her through gritted teeth.

I saw Victoria's jaw clench, a wild look re-entering her eyes. In that moment I knew that no matter what code of honour she abided by, she was going to kill James.

I immediately ran towards him, but I was too late and she lunged forwards.


Although I had been too late to save him, Lucien hadn't.

He threw himself into James, throwing him clear of Victoria's attack, and although James was safe, Lucien hadn't been so lucky:

The world seemed to pass in slow motion as her hand thrust deep into his chest and her monstrous fangs locked around his throat.

Just then, the world returned to its normal pace as she snapped her head back and pulled her hand out of his chest, in unison.

Both attacks claimed a prize: A still beating heart, and a mixture of bloody bone and flesh.


Lucien's lifeless body fell to the ground and I wrapped my arms around Helena, restraining her as she let out a pained howl and began sobbing.

"NO!" She screamed, fighting against me, pulling in the direction of her fallen partner. "No!" She repeated, weaker this time, her sobs filling her throat as she fell down into my arms. I crouched down to the floor with her, my arms still wrapped tightly around her, but now they were in a comforting position, her face angled towards Lucien's corpse.

Victoria released one final pained sigh as the blood of her son ran down her throat, killing instantly.

# CHAPTER TEN

The days that followed were some of the darkest, silent ones that I had ever experienced.

We hadn't only lost Lucien that evening.

Victoria knew that she was going to die that day, so that was why she had broken her code of honour:

We found Elaine's mutilated body within the shredded mattress of her bed.

We found Marius's twisted, bloody form beside a large, still pond where, centuries previous, he and Victoria had performed their wedding vows.

The only one left of her blood line was James, and the reason that he was still alive was because of the sacrifice and interception of his brother.

He had not been the same since that day as a newfound exhausted fury resided in the place where his compassion once was.

He had stopped singing.

The band had fallen apart.

Their fans believed them to be dead, and they were correct as the soul of 'Your Last Goodbye' had indeed been quenched like a flame beneath a cascading flood of blood from his brother, father and aunt.

James never once left the darkness of his room where he sat on his bed, motionless.

Isaac, Helena and I all had to repeatedly inject him with human blood, daily, to keep him from starving. But as the weeks and months went on we realised that it was no way for him to live and as we were considering letting him succumb to the death that he so desired, one evening, we heard a knock on the large, Oak door of the mansion.

There, on the doorstep, stood a girl of around the age of nineteen, with straight, light brown hair and a mousy nose. She wore a cute, short, purple dress and looked at me with a distraught expression as she stood there.

I gave her a sad smile as I recognised her eyes.

"Layla." I said kindly, reaching forward and wrapping my arms around her. She began crying and hugged me back.

I knew why she was here: Layla would have heard of Victoria's death and would have hence learnt of her freedom. But with the death of her master, she would also have heard about the death of her mother, Elaine, and she was here to mourn her.

I pulled her into the building and walked her over to the dining room table that, all those months ago, I had been laid upon and lost my false humanity at the hands of Irina. Within less than a day of consuming my blood, she had also passed away.

I turned the chair so that it was facing away from the table and as I sat her down, I crouched in front of her.

She continued to sob as I looked over her pale face.

Layla was an orphan, just like Helena and myself... it was our duty to keep her safe.

Just then my sister walked into the room and stood beside me, staring at the girl weeping. Exactly as I had done previously, she made the connection with Elaine and joined me on the ground, waiting for her to cease her crying enough to speak.

She looked at us with wet eyes and furrowed brows and asked, weakly "Where is she?"

Helena and I both looked to each other and decided that it was time.

Together, we rose from the ground, and each taking one of Layla's arms, we led her from the room.

It was time to plan the funeral for those we had lost.


*Two days later*

*Knock knock*

I slowly entered James's room, expecting his heavy curtains to be drawn, and for him to be sat motionless in bed, but he wasn't.

I was surprised to see him stood by his full length mirror, fastening a tie.

I closed the door and slowly walked over to him.

"James?"

He didn't turn; he merely moved his gaze slightly from his chest and into the mirror, looking at my reflection.

His wearied, exhausted, hollow eyes met mine and I sighed, crossing the remainder of the space between us in no time at all, wrapping my arms around his waist.

At first he stood rigid and didn't respond to my touch, but I continued to hold him, squeezing him tighter in an attempt to cure him of his grief and bring him back to who he once was.

My mind flashed through all of the events in my life that had involved him; when the sound of his music had saved me and brought me back from the edge of my grief of Helena and my father; meeting him –the false memory and the correct one, both of which I had believed to have brought us closer-; how he was willing to confront the monster that was his mother with the simple aim of making me feel as though I wasn't alone; the way he had held me when he realised that I was still alive...

After all of this, I realised that I had fallen in love with him.

A love that burned so deeply that if it wasn't reciprocated, I would be crushed and I would have lost *yet another person*... I held him tighter to me, begging with my mind for him to come back and when I felt him move and place his hands around my waist, I crumbled at his touch and fell into him.

He then held me tighter, pushing me closer to him and after a few moments of not saying anything, I pulled back.

"James." I began, tears in my eyes, but before I could continue he had placed his right hand on my cheek and brought his mouth to mine.

The shock that had once erupted between the two of us sparked up again like a newly lit fire, engulfing us both in the heat of the moment.

I pulled back, drawing in a large breath, feeling as though I had been kissed for the first time and as I was about to say something, he grabbed the back of my head and pulled me closer towards him, kissing me hard and pushing me back against the wall. I pressed both hands on the back of his blazer as he pushed me further into the stone, gripping my face tightly.


(Helena)

I slowly walked into the room where the bodies were held, and after ensuring that I was alone, I made my way over to Lucien's open coffin.

He had been dressed in a high necked shirt and blazer, coupled with a blue tie that had matched his beautifully pale eyes perfectly.

I didn't try to stop the tears as they fell, remembering the times we had shared together; our first kiss...;the moment he had first told me that he loved me...

I cried hard as the memories came flooding back, reaching forward and placing my palm on his ice cold jaw.

"No..." I whispered, bowing my head. I clenched my teeth together in an attempt to stop my loud sobs, and I placed both hands on the side of the mahogany coffin, gripping the wood hard.

I released it and turned around, sliding down the stone plinth to fall to the floor, bringing my knees up and wrapping my arms around them, the tears still profusely forcing themselves down my face.

(Layla)

Today was the day... I was going to see my mother again after all these years.

Victoria was dead. That was meant to be what sparked our reunion that I had been dreaming about for so long...

Seeing her cold dead corpse in a coffin was not what I had envisaged.

I perched on the edge of my lilac quilted bed, twisting the pendant that my mother had given me, around my fingers, staring at the long black dress that hung from the back of my door.

But I had to do this for her... I had to say goodbye... One last goodbye...

With a deep breath, I rose and slowly walked over to the lacy garment.

I ran my fingers over its surface, closing my eyes and imagining my mother stood behind me, smiling encouragingly.

I opened my eyes and reached the article of clothing down from its hook, my hands shaking as I slipped it over my skin.

I stood in front of my mirror, gazing emptily at my appearance, but I could not enjoy the beauty of what I was wearing as it was only ever going to be a reminder of what I had lost: My mother and father who had been killed by the woman that had enslaved me for the past ten years.

I could never forget...

(Isaac)

I stood in my bathroom, adjusting the burgundy tie that hung about my neck and I looked into my own aged eyes.

"C'mon old boy. One more funeral."

You'd think that after the many years of having to attend my mortal friend's funerals and those of my human family, through the generations, I would have grown a slight immunity to the pain it ensued, but alas, that was not how grief worked: You could never be prepared for it, and it would never get easier.

I had known Marius since my first day of being here one hundred and eighty years ago... He had been my closest, dearest friend and now he was gone: Torn apart by his wife, whom he would admit to no-one, not even himself, that he still loved. Even after everything she had done, he still held a shred of hope that the woman he had married was buried somewhere beneath her murderous shell. A lot of people had protested against her being at the funeral, but once upon a time she had been a pure, loving woman, and she was to be put to rest in the family crypt with both Marius and Lucien.

*Later that day*
(Lucy)

We had all gathered in the room which held our loved ones and as we mourned, preparations were being made outside: Tall, fiery torches were being placed in the ground to line the path to the Killoran crypt and the main graveyard. The digging of my mother's grave was also an important task that had to be completed.

Ten minutes later, Simon returned and addressed us all.

"Everyone." He began, his broad Scottish accent coming through strongly. "It's time."

Helena and I both walked towards my mother's coffin.

We both gazed over her pale, lifeless face for one last time before we closed the lid, exchanging a heart broken, tear stricken look over the mahogany shell that was to be my mother's home for eternity.

We then proceeded to lift the coffin onto our shoulders and we walked forwards, followed by the others as we slowly travelled through the double doors, out into the darkness of the garden.

We both kept our backs straight and our eyes forward, not once looking down: We needed to transport her safely to her grave and *then* we could truly mourn for her as we lowered her coffin into the ground. But not now.

The journey from the house appeared to last for a short eternity, the weight of her coffin appearing to increase as the seconds went by, but I knew this added weight was the impending sense of dread that flooded my body at the fear of seeing her named carved into a marble headstone: Because that was when it would be finalised. Right now, I could shake the thought away, almost as if I didn't see her dead body, then it couldn't be true and she was just somewhere else. But once I saw her name in that unforgiving, unyielding stone, then she would be gone.

She would be dead and Helena and I would be orphans.

We turned the corner and I almost stopped at the sight of it.

There it was, ten metres ahead: The grave of my mother.

As we neared the cold, white marble, I read the inscription, feeling the tears force their way into my eyes:

*Sarah Amilia Brown,*
*Aged 42*
*2nd April 1973 – 5th June 2015*
*Beloved mother and friend,*
*Tragically killed,*
*You will remain in our hearts,*
*Forever and Always*

The skin on my shoulder that held my tattoo tensed as I read the final line:

'*Forever and Always*'...

The second we reached the grave, I could feel my tears forcing their way down my face, yet I still refused to let the sadness take me over as we lowered her on top of two big, thick black ropes.

Helena, James, Isaac and I all took one side of each rope. I remained level-headed as Helena and I locked eyes over the coffin that housed our mother, nodded grimly, took a deep breath in unison, and then all four of us lowered her into the ground.

James and Isaac returned to the crowd of Vampires, not saying a word, and Helena and I proceeded to walk to the mound of dirt at the base of her grave, picking up a handful each.

I felt the sobs crawling up my throat as I stood next to her grave, my hand outstretched and clenched, holding the dirt.

"Ashes to ashes." I breathed, my throat hoarse, tears streaming down my face as I slowly let the fine grains of soil drift through my fingers.

"Dust to dust." Helena echoed in the same tone, as she too released a handful of dirt onto the wooden coffin that made a slight scratching sound as it landed.

We turned to each other before looking down at our mother's new home. More tears began to fall with each second that passed and I placed my arm around Helena's waist, turning her to me. Returning my embrace, she buried her face in my shoulder, shaking with the tears that wracked her body. I too felt my own tears falling but today I had to be strong for my sister so I held her tight and close to me, closing my eyes, thankful that I could be here with and for her.

"Hey, Helena?" I asked, pulling back.

"Yeah?" She choked. Her red, watery, tired eyes met mine. Placing my right hand into the small pocket of my dress, I brought out a silver chain. Helena frowned in confusion for a moment, but a second later a small smile crossed her features. "My necklace."

"Yeah, it is." I gave her a comforting smile before walking to stand behind her, placing the chain over her head and connecting the two thin pieces of silver.

She turned to face me and once again wrapped her arms around me.

When she pulled back I looked down at her pendant.

"You're whole again now." She gave me another watery smile and laughed lightly.

"Yeah. I am." Her expression fell and she turned to our mother's grave. "One piece of my life may have been returned to me, but two pieces of my heart have been torn out." He breathed, wrapping her hand around the onyx pendant.

"I know." I replied quietly, a grim expression crossing my own face. "But we do what we always do." My eyes took on a hard appearance. "We survive. But this time we have each other." I once again wrapped my arms around her and pulled her tightly towards me before we both walked back to the crowd of Vampires behind us.

Helena returned to stand with Isaac and I took my place next to James, looking with dead eyes at the hole within the ground. Once I had returned to my position of standing by his side, James put his hand in the centre of my back and then wrapped it around my waist, pulling me towards him. I leant my head on his shoulder and closed my eyes as I heard Simon force the shovel into the mound of earth at the base of her grave. I winced upon hearing the dirt make contact with the top of the coffin.

As the minutes passed, the deathly silence was almost too much to bear. It was only broken by the repeated grating and thudding sounds of the metal shovel collecting the dirt, and then dispersing it onto the coffin, constantly reminding me of my mother's death. Upon sensing my discomfort Isaac walked up to stand in front of her grave.

"Sarah Brown–" He began, and my heart tightened at the mention of her name "–was a wonderful woman who I am very proud to have had the privilege to meet. Now she can be reunited with your father who, unfortunately, I never had the chance to see. But girls–" He addressed the two of us. "–know that they would be extremely happy and proud of how far you have both come. I would also like to thank them for blessing us with the two of you. I know–" His eyes met James's "–we would all feel incomplete if you weren't here. These two women standing here are a pair of the strongest, most caring people I have ever met. From experience I also know you're both extremely stubborn and opinionated-" He gave us both a small smile and I felt myself chuckle lightly in response to his statement "-but that just adds to the fire that lies within you both, making you even more unique and amazing people. So Sarah." He turned to face her headstone just as Simon had finished filling the gaping hole in the ground "Until the day I die, I swear I will do my best to protect them both."

He then walked to the right of the crowd and removed a single red rose from a black wicker basket and laid it to rest on my mother's grave, returning to his position beside Helena moments later.

She gave him a small, tear ridden smile as she passed him to select her own rose.

Following suit, I walked gently across the ground and joined Helena by our mother's grave, the ruby petals of our roses appearing bright and full of life in the light of the fiery torches that surrounded us.

In unison we both bent down and placed them upon the uneven ground, our eyes dry from the tears that we could no longer produce.

Taking my hand, James and I led the crowd of silent Vampires back into the house. He released me upon seeing his brother's coffin and I sensed him tense, seeing his jaw clench as he struggled to hold back his own tears. With shaking hands he and another Vampire lifted the wooden case up onto their shoulders. James halted for a moment, closing his eyes and taking a deep breath, before opening them again, placing his hand against the wood and walking out of the room. Closely behind him walked Simon and Layla, supporting Elaine's identical casket. Layla's eyes met mine as she passed and I attempted to give her a supportive, caring smile as she passed through the doors. Two Vampires that I didn't recognise chose Victoria's coffin, not disguising their disgust well as they mounted the wood onto their shoulders and followed the others out of the room.

Josh, Damian, Chris, and Ben all walked closely behind them, each carrying the equipment for their instruments.

I frowned in confusion but I was too mentally exhausted to ask any questions.

Helena stood by my side as we followed the coffins and the band down the dirt path towards the Killoran crypt.

She turned to me "Hey Luc, how are you doing?"

I gave her a small, watery smile and replied with "Coping."

She nodded in agreement and that was the only form of verbal communication we made as we continued trailing the coffin bearers, our eyes locked straight ahead, wanting this day to be over as fast as possible.

We finally arrived at the stone crypt and Damian laid his guitar on the ground, gently opening the door. The Vampires supporting the coffins entered, placing the wooden caskets down in their allocated places. They all silently exited the small building, with Damian closing the door behind them.

Up until this point, James had not said anything nor had he shown any intention of doing so until he stood in front of the door to the crypt and addressed us all, his hands joined in front of him.

"Today I will not read a eulogy for my fallen father or brother." I saw his jaw clench in his attempts to quench the overwhelming sadness that I knew resided in his chest "Nor for my aunt or her sister." I noticed how he hadn't mentioned Victoria's relation to him, but I didn't blame him as it was she who had killed everyone else that we were laying to rest today. "Instead, I will do something that I believe will reach them the most, and probably what they would have wanted and expected from me on this day." He took a deep breath "This song is for those we have lost and for those that were left behind." He locked eyes with me "This is 'Your Last Goodbye'." He finished before falling silent.

Of course...

This song would be extremely important to him today, no wonder he named it after his band that he had nurtured and grown with over the years.

The song began with a slow, melodious tune, Damian expertly pressing his fingers into the neck of his guitar, the sound echoing around the dark silence.

After a few moments, James began singing; his deep voice slightly coarse from the tears that I knew would be crawling up his throat.

*The time has come,*
*The curtain falls,*
*Now you've gone*
*and left us all.*
*Your soul will live on,*
*In the hearts of everyone,*
*The mark that you made,*
*Will never fade away.*
*Now that it's time,*
*For your last goodbye,*
*There are so many souls,*
*That'll scream your battle cry!*
*Today is done,*
*The wounds are sealed,*
*The pain is gone,*
*But scars remain.*
*You gave it all,*
*But not in vain.*
*Now that it's time,*
*For your last goodbye,*
*We must carry on,*
*Turning a blind eye.*
*The battle's won,*

*The thieves are dead,*
*Yet demons run,*
*and fill our souls with dread.*
*So lay your head to rest,*
*Know that we loved you best,*
*and that we will miss you more*
*than we can ever scream!*
*Now that it's time...*
*For your last goodbye...*
*Know that I'll say your name,*
*'Till the day that I die...*

On the last word, James's voice broke and reflected in the light of the flaming torches around us, I could see the tears lining his face. I saw that his jaw was clenched from stopping his cries from becoming audible and he slowly made his way towards me.

Looking into James's eyes, I realised that mourning those we have lost can help us heal and can also pull us back from the brink of darkness because we have a reason to live: Telling their story and living as they would have wanted. I knew it would take us all a long time to get used to and be comfortable within our own lives, lacking those we had lost, but I knew we would make it through.

That was the beauty of living for an eternity: The one thing that we would never be short of was time.

From that day forwards James, Damian, Josh, Ben and Chris took the whole world by storm, fuelled by their new surge of power that burnt within them in each show, causing their instruments to sound even more beautiful and meaningful than before, saving more people like me. They had all experienced a fresh wave of loss and pain, James especially, so they all immediately transferred those feelings into lyrics, chord patterns, and drum beats.

From all of the feedback they received, I knew that those who supported 'Your Last Goodbye' could tell something had happened within all five of their lives. Even though I was now in a relationship with a member of the band, and close friends with the other four, I was still part of the gigantic family that supported them. Sometimes I went to a few of their shows and talked to the leather clad, black haired fans that had their own powerful, meaningful stories to tell, and all six of us offered support where we could, reminding them that they were never alone. All five of them saved me from the darkest places of my life so now it was my turn to assist them in doing the same for other people.

The beauty of pain and despair is that you come out the other side stronger: You've fought the darkness, won the battle and *survived*. I knew that lot of other people had their own struggles and sometimes they didn't receive the support they needed from their friends or family, so the music 'Your Last Goodbye' created and all five of the men that made up the band were the support they needed to make it through: To see another dawn and live another day. Now I was within the band members' world, I knew that all they ever wanted was to help and be that light in the darkness for those who were being suffocated by the horrors, disappointments and pain of life.

I realised that up until this point, I believed that this world was controlled by humans but I was wrong.

The events that had occurred in my life over the past few months had caused me to realise that *Vampires* are in fact the ones that have control of this world because they have lived in it long enough to see the greed, impatience and cruelty that humans possess. They have risen above it, becoming the *higher beings* of this world. Vampires are seen to be 'godless creatures' and that is why they have been 'cursed to the shadows', but that is not the case, quite the contrary: They hide in the shadows because they *know* the darkness of this world so they complete little, subtle acts of kindness that give the youth of this time the belief that there is some hope, some light, and some *good* in this world. We do this so they can hopefully make a better future for themselves, eradicating the sadness and animosity that some humans have created between each other; wars; segregation; murder and other crimes that leave people paralysed with pain.

I have come to one conclusion:

This is not the Age of Man...
This is the Age of Vampires.

# ACKNOWLEDGEMENTS

I am aware that most acknowledgement sections within novels are between one and two pages in length, but as I have received so much support, I simply have a lot of people to thank. So the following pages are filled with the words that hold a sense of massive appreciation for those around me.

I am aware that most acknowledgment sections within novels are between one and two pages in length, but as I have received so much support, I simply have a lot of people to thank. The following pages are filled with the words that hold a sense of massive appreciation for those around me.

Although every single one of my friends and each member of my family have been extremely supportive throughout the creation of this novel, listed below are those that I especially want to thank:

Andrew (Goose) Exley – A boy who has always cheered me up when I needed it and who has also been one of my closest friends.

Charlotte Reardon – The girl who has honestly been my dearest, best friend for as long back as I can remember.

Maxwell Lawrence – Although at times my ability to write 50,000 words has confused him immensely, he has been such a loving, funny, supportive friend and boyfriend throughout this whole experience. I want to really thank him for the fact that he has always been able to tolerate me at my worst, keeping me together so we can be happy when I'm at my best.

Now it would be seen as very strange to do this as most students *despise* their teachers, but I wanted to mention two people who have been extremely helpful and caring throughout my entire education at my current school:

Ms. McDonnell – My English teacher who has always been very entertaining. She also awarded me the only 'A' that I have *ever* achieved within my work and it was on a short story that I wrote, adding to my confidence within this career path.

Mr. Bancroft – My Film Studies teacher who I have always been able to have a laugh with, but I am also greatly in awe of just *how* wise and knowledgeable he is. I am very passionate about film and everything that I have learnt, and everything I will ever achieve within the film industry, I owe to this man.

I would also like to thank a number of specific members of my family:

Louise Wallinger – My Godmother who has been the closest person to an aunt I have ever known. She has always supported me through everything I have ever done in my life, and has constantly been the one to bring a smile to my face at times when I really needed it.

Caroline Bond (my mother) & Andrew Bond (my step-father) – These two people have been the ones who have seen me all the time, seven days a week, and throughout every day they have always given me the useful and truthful advice I have needed. I really would like to thank them for coping with my many fiery 'tantrums' and also for raising me well, because even though I have three younger brothers, they have always managed to make time for me. At times I felt as though I *hated* them for their harsh words of reality, but looking back in retrospect, those lessons really had a helping hand in shaping me into the person I am today. At the time of writing and publishing this novel, I am within my last full year of living beneath their roof, before I move out to pursue my adult life. So I want to officially show my appreciation for them being able to cope with me all these years and for being the best parents I could ever have wished for.

My Nana and Grandpa – My grandparents have been extremely important and influential people in my life. When I was younger, my Nana always used to say that she would 'spoil' me, but never 'rot' me. Although this may not make any sense to an outsider, I now see its significance:

She always used to 'spoil' me by buying me sweets and taking me shopping, every year, in Mevagissey harbour. But she never 'rotted' me as she always put a limit on how many sweets I could eat a day and always restricted what I could buy and any one time. At the time I hated it. But now I know that she did it to make me humble and appreciative of everything and everyone around me. I also want to thank my Nana for being the woman who really got me interested in reading and writing stories from a young age. I know for a fact that I wouldn't be where I am today without her. My Grandpa also deserves a very special mention for his ability to tolerate my Nana when she is confronted with an issue within modern technology, and let's not forget the 'frozen pork chop' incident!

Then there are my three younger brothers: Indy, Henry and Daniel (who were aged seven, six and three at the time I wrote this novel) who constantly gave me big cuddles and also woke me up at unholy times in the morning, ruining my sleeping pattern!

One large group of people that I would also like to mention is the YouTube community and all of my brilliant subscribers who have remained loyal and friendly over the past year of me creating my videos.

The one band that has made the completion of this book possible has been 'Black Veil Brides'.

Andy Biersack, Ashley Purdy, Jake Pitts, Christian 'CC' Coma, and Jinxx are the five men who have created the music that has fuelled my imagination and greatly influenced the writing of this novel. Also, during a few dark periods that I experienced in the time that this book was being created, this band's music has helped me overcome my sadness and anger and has caused me to come out stronger the other side. For that I could never thank them enough.

Finally, the last and possibly the most important person that I would like to thank is my father, Neil Petford.

I remember when I was younger, around the age of nine, I had begun to write a short story called 'The Magic Lake'. All the while I was writing it, he refused to read it until it was complete. Unfortunately he died when I was ten years old so he was never able to read it. From that day forward, I vowed that that first book I ever completed and published would be in memory of him, as he was such an amazing, highly influential person in the decade of my life that he raised me.

# ABOUT THE AUTHOR

Sophie Petford is a seventeen year old girl who currently resides in Derbyshire (UK) with her mother, step-father, and three younger brothers. In a year she hopes to study film at University, moving on to pursue a career within television/film acting – while writing more novels on the side. Sophie also greatly enjoys rock music, pizza, and horror films. As is evident by the nature of this novel, she has an unhealthy obsession with mythology.

www.sophiepetford.com

43041060R10112

Made in the USA
Charleston, SC
11 June 2015